"I'm going to be a father. Break out the cigars!"

"No, Patrick. *I'm* having a baby. I'm having this baby, and I don't think you should be involved."

"I don't see how I can be any less involved."

"I meant—" Kate paused and took a deep breath. "My baby *is* going to have a father. But it won't be you."

"It's a little too late to make that choice, Kate. I *am* the father."

She shook her head. "Not in that way."

"Oh? So who is the father *in that way?*"

"I've got a list of possibilities, but I—"

"A list! And I'm not on it?" With a laugh, he leaned back against the workbench. "What kind of joke is this?"

Dear Reader,

For years I have been fascinated with ocean racing. What makes racers tick? Why do they go out and push themselves and their boats to the limits of endurance and beyond? And if disaster strikes and they are rescued, why do they go out and do it again? From the outside—even to a sailor like myself—that kind of racing looks crazy. But a sexy confidence, a bold swagger, runs among this breed of racers, the sort that can look attractive to a woman standing safely on the shore.

The inspiration for this book came from wondering what love was like for these exceptional men. Some must have girlfriends waiting for them at home. Some even have homes and families. From there, *Baby on Board* began to take shape. I hope you enjoy reading about Patrick and Kate and the choices they have to make to find happiness.

Please visit me at www.lisaruff.net. And keep a watch out for my next book!

Happy reading,

Lisa Ruff

Baby on Board

LISA RUFF

TORONTO • NEW YORK • LONDON
AMSTERDAM • PARIS • SYDNEY • HAMBURG
STOCKHOLM • ATHENS • TOKYO • MILAN • MADRID
PRAGUE • WARSAW • BUDAPEST • AUCKLAND

Recycling programs
for this product may
not exist in your area.

ISBN-13: 978-0-373-75247-8
ISBN-10:   0-373-75247-4

BABY ON BOARD

Copyright © 2009 by Lisa Ruff.

www.eHarlequin.com

Printed in U.S.A.

ABOUT THE AUTHOR

Lisa Ruff was born in Montana and grew up in Idaho but met the man of her dreams in Seattle. She married Kirk promising to love, honor and edit his rough drafts. His pursuit of writing led Lisa to the craft. A longtime reader of romance, she decided to try to create one herself. The first version of *Man of the Year* took three months to finish, but her day job got in the way of polishing the manuscript. She stuffed it into a drawer, where it languished for several years.

In pursuit of time to write and freedom to explore the world, Lisa, Kirk and their cat sailed from Seattle on a thirty-seven-foot boat. They spent five years cruising in Central America and the Caribbean. Lisa wrote romance, but it took a backseat to an adventurous life. She was busy writing travel essays, learning to speak Spanish from taxi drivers and handling a small boat in gale-force winds.

When she returned to land life, she finally revised *Man of the Year* and sent it to an agent. Within a year, she had a contract from Harlequin American Romance.

She and her husband are cruising on a sailboat again somewhere in the Atlantic Ocean. When not setting sail for another port, she is working on her next Harlequin romance.

Books by Lisa Ruff

HARLEQUIN AMERICAN ROMANCE

1214—MAN OF THE YEAR

To sailors and those who love them:
fair winds and following seas.

Chapter One

A shadow shifted across the room, startling Kate. The heart-shaped glass bubble she held slipped, fell to the steel table with a crack, then shattered into a hundred red shards. A strangled cry of distress escaped from between her lips. She put her hands out, as if to gather the pieces back into a whole, but knew there was no saving it. She lifted her eyes to the figure standing in the doorway, limned by the afternoon sun.

"Damn it, Patrick! Can't you at least knock?"

The tall, dark-haired man moved around the worktable. His tanned face held a crooked, teasing smile that invited her to play. At the sight of it, the studio felt ten degrees hotter than before. The quick beat of her pulse could come from fright, but she knew that wasn't the cause. Patrick Berzani was reason enough.

"After three months at sea, you'd think I'd get a better welcome than that."

Low and intimate, his voice raised a shiver across her skin. He sounded amused that he had startled her, but she could also hear desire threaded through his words. The combination unlocked the lid on memories that Kate thought she had banished forever: their first cup of coffee at the café, his long-lashed, silver-gray eyes looking at her with warm interest, his curly black hair splayed across her pillow, begging to be touched. She tried in vain to stuff all these images back where they belonged. She had spent months forgetting them—and *him*—and thought she had succeeded. How could all that effort disappear like smoke?

The smile, the eyes, his hair, even the golden earring, high in the curve of his left ear, had deceived her from the start. Patrick had laughed when she asked if he was an artist like her. No, he was a sailor—a racer—whose only experience painting was on the hull of a sailboat. The earring was from a trip around Cape Horn. Later, after they were lovers, she learned other things: he got the tattoo around his arm after his first voyage across the equator, wore boat shoes for all occasions and always had string and a rigging knife in his pocket for emergency repairs.

Dragging herself back to the present, she drew a deep breath. "It's the only kind of welcome you deserve, scaring me like that." She meant to sound harsh and angry. Enough so that he would take his captivating smile and beautiful eyes far away, but her voice came out husky instead. She heard the want, the need, all too clearly.

She knew Patrick heard it, too. He didn't pause a single step. He held her eyes with his. Kate's feet were rooted to the floor as if encased in the concrete. The furnace behind her, with its bubbling pot of molten glass, roared and huffed, echoing the turmoil inside her. Glass globes hanging from the ceiling caught the sunlight from the windows. A kaleidoscope of colors—cyan, turquoise, amber and lemon—shimmered around the room, creating more confusion.

When he reached out, her more rational half asserted itself briefly. If he touched her, she would be lost. She grabbed a brush and dustpan from under the table.

"I have to clean up the mess you—"

"Later." He cupped her face in his hands and stopped her words with a soft, hungry kiss.

His warm mouth captured hers as his arms encircled her, drawing her close to his tall, muscular body. The dustpan and brush slipped from her grip and clattered to the floor as she wrapped herself around him like molten glass onto a punty. Kate was flooded with the flavor and scent of Patrick Berzani. She felt as though she was drowning when she was in his arms. But she wasn't afraid, not the way she was around water. This drowning was exhilarating, spinning her, engulfing her with pleasure, daring her to descend into the depths where she should not go.

A slight fluttering in her abdomen, the faintest of sensations, brought her back to reality. She wrenched her lips from his. "Patrick, wait." Her voice was breathless. Desire coursed through her body, expecting fulfillment. Patrick's eyes, their silver-gray darkened to pewter, didn't calm her.

"Katie." He brushed a hand over her cheek and back into her hair. The blue bandanna wrapped around her head dropped to the floor. Her hair sprang free of confinement as his fingers delved into the mass of curls. "It's been too long."

Cupping the back of her neck, he bent his head to give her another intense, drugging kiss. Kate began to slide under his spell again. She fought free and put a hand on his chest, twisting away before their bodies could make contact again.

"Wait a minute. This is going way too fast."

"It's not going nearly fast enough." He reached for her again.

Kate evaded his grasp. "I've got a piece working right now. I can't just leave it."

"Sure you can." Patrick's wicked smile coaxed her. "You've done it before."

She smiled back at him—she couldn't help it—but shook her head. "This time I can't."

"All those weeks at sea, I thought of you."

His words shored up her shaky resolve, reminding her that he had left her alone for some time, reminding her why she should be rid of this man. "Well, you'll just have to do more thinking."

She stepped around the worktable. Six feet in length and steel topped, it was only a temporary barricade against him. Even the long metal arms at the end of the bench, where she rolled her blowpipe, were poor barriers. What she needed was a defense. She could use one of the glass rods on the table like a foil to fend him off. Or the torch she used for melding glass. It burned at over five thousand degrees, surely hotter than her passion for this man. There were plenty of weapons at her disposal in the studio. Not one of them could guard her heart.

The baby in her womb kicked, as if to tell Kate that she was not the only one agitated by this man. She took a deep breath and resisted the urge to press a hand to the slight protrusion. Instead, she took a wide paintbrush and swept the broken glass onto a tray. She wasn't going back around the table for the hand broom and dustpan. It was too dangerous over there, for a number of reasons. Patrick's eyes followed her, but he stayed where he was, perching himself on a stool at his side of the table.

"Sorry about making you break that glass."

Kate kept her back to him as she dumped the broken pieces of the heart into the melt bin. "It's not the first time it's been broken," she said, and swallowed down the tears that sprang to her eyes.

When she turned around, Patrick was watching her closely, his head tilted, eyes narrowed.

She cleared her throat and smiled a little. "I mean, it's

not the first piece of glass I've ever broken. It won't be the last." Moving over to a large oven—the "garage" that kept glass pieces in progress hot—Kate extracted another glass bubble with a lustrous blue sheen and brought it to the worktable. Setting it on a ceramic-fiber blanket, she pulled out paint and a brush. She could feel Patrick's eyes on her as she worked.

"When did you get back?"

"Yesterday. Actually, it was early this morning." He smiled. "I came right over to see you."

Kate arched an eyebrow and looked at her watch. "It's three o'clock in the afternoon."

"A man's got to sleep doesn't he?"

"You hardly ever sleep. I bet you were sailing." When he grinned, Kate knew she had guessed correctly. "Don't you ever get tired of it? You just spent three months racing a boat on the ocean and within twenty-four hours you're out on another one."

"Different boat, different sailing." Patrick shrugged. "A wind junkie's got to get his fix."

She shook her head. He always said the same thing, whatever version of the question she asked. She didn't understand him any better today than she had five months ago when they first met. Picking up the warm, delicate sphere by the punty, she brushed dark blue paint onto it in a spiraling pattern.

"What's that?" Patrick asked.

"A new paint I'm experimenting with. It keeps its color better after it's fired." She kept her eyes focused on her task, pretending to ignore him. Her hands trembled slightly as she wielded the brush. She concentrated on the glass in her hand, but her lines were as wavy as if she were painting on a boat at sea. She set the globe down for a moment and went to the furnace, peering into the crucible.

She checked the gauges and turned one knob up a notch while dialing down another to adjust the heat and flame. The small act of control settled her nerves a little. She went back to the table and took up brush and globe once again. This time, her lines were better, more smooth and even.

Patrick came around the workbench and stood next to her. He trailed a finger down her cheek. She raised startled eyes to his. The design on the glass ended in a blob of paint.

"I missed you, Katie." His voice was soft and caressing. "Did you miss me?"

"Every now and then." The brush that slipped from her fingers and fell to the table belied her casual words.

With an internal curse, she stiffened her spine and evaded another touch by turning back to the furnace, settling the piece inside the garage to rest in the heat. She would finish it when her head was clearer, when Patrick was gone. Surreptitiously, Kate smoothed a hand over her abdomen. This child was more than enough reason to send Patrick on his way, but how? She could tell him that she was needed in the shop in front of the house, but he might remember it was closed on Mondays. She couldn't hope for an interruption from Molly, either, since she was in Santa Fe.

She kept her distance from Patrick, aligning a few pieces of flat, dichroic glass that were already in tidy rows. She moved back to the other side of the table, keeping the barrier between them. "How long are you here this time?"

"That depends." Patrick followed her around the table and leaned against the bench, his hands braced on the edge.

"On what?" Kate just barely kept herself from making the circuit to the other side of the table again. She could imagine him chasing her around it all afternoon.

"I've got a couple of new boats to run some trials on." He picked up a rod of deep green glass from the workbench, twirling it between his fingers. "It depends on you, too."

Kate bent down to the floor and picked up her bandanna and the brush and dustpan. His casual attitude grated. After those months apart, did he actually think they could just pick up where they had left off? Whether he knew it or not, things had changed.

"Really? It never has before."

Patrick raised a brow. "I thought you'd want to spend some time together before I leave for the Trans-Oceana race."

Kate shoved the bandanna into the back pocket of her jeans and tossed the brush onto the shelf under the table. "I'd have to rearrange my schedule."

"Your schedule was never a problem before."

She turned and met his eyes with a frosty stare. "It's been three *months*, Patrick. I didn't think I'd see you again."

"Why would you think that?" He looked puzzled. He put the glass tube down and walked over to rest his hands on her shoulders. Close enough to kiss, his lips lifted in a slight smile. "I told you that I'd be back."

"Then why didn't I hear from you?" Kate watched him closely as she asked the question.

"I called you," Patrick said with a slight frown.

"Once! One call."

"I was in the middle of the Atlantic—"

"Don't try to tell me you were cut off from all communication, Patrick." Kate threw up her hands and spun away from him, away from his touch. If she didn't put some distance between them, she would strangle him. "Everything you did—everything you *said*—was posted on the race Web site every day."

"I didn't write that," Patrick said in protest. "I was sailing the boat. The sponsor put some guy on board with a satellite phone. He did all the updates."

"What about before, then? The race took *three weeks*. You called me when you first got to France, but you didn't leave the dock for weeks after that. You could have let me know you were all right, or asked me how I was doing. Did you even think about me *once* while you were gone?"

"I did. Honest." Patrick faced her squarely. "But it's crazy before the race. There's never enough time to get everything done. Something always goes wrong at the last minute."

"There were photos of you on the boat, on the docks and at lots of parties, Patrick." She shot him a glare. "You looked really *busy* with a beer in your hand."

Patrick ran a hand through his hair. "Katie, I—"

"I never even crossed your mind, did I?" She searched his eyes. What she saw there deflated her anger, filling her with sadness.

Patrick fell silent, his face somber now. Finally, he raised his hands in a gesture of defeat. "I'm sorry. I should have called more."

Kate sighed. The apology only depressed her. She had handled this poorly. She had let anger take control, when she should have been calm. Of course, she had never planned to have this conversation with Patrick, but that was no excuse. It was time to end this once and for all.

"Yes, you should have, but that's beside the point." Kate rubbed a hand over her forehead. "It was over between us when you left. I—"

"It was?" His laugh was short and sharp. "We spent every night together for the last month. Did I miss something?"

Kate flushed, remembering all too well the passion

they had shared. "I should have known it after the first week you were gone, when I didn't hear from you again. When I saw what a good time you were having," she continued, ignoring his interruption.

"I'm *sorry,* Kate." Patrick reached to take her in his arms. "We can start over."

"No, we can't." She stepped out of range.

"Sure we can."

"We had an affair." She sat on the stool and leaned an elbow against the table, shoulders slumped. "I thought it was more, but three months of silence taught me a lesson. It was just an affair."

Kate met Patrick's eyes. The gray had somehow turned to silver again, hiding his thoughts. That clear color was the perfect camouflage. Like water, it reflected its surroundings, never revealing what lay beneath.

"So what do you want?"

Kate swallowed hard. The words she had to speak were painful. "I want you to leave. I'll stay here and work, and we'll both get on with our lives."

"No, it doesn't end like this. It's too good between us."

Kate stood and faced him. This was possibly the hardest thing she had ever had to do. More than anything, she wanted to go to him and press herself against his strong body. She wanted—ached—to feel his arms close around her as he held her tight. But she wouldn't. She couldn't just think of herself. Not anymore. She stiffened her spine.

"We had a good time, Patrick. But that's over."

He looked at her silently, his expression a carefully controlled mask. Some indefinable emotion swept through his eyes, turning them a dark and stormy gray. "I can't believe you mean that."

"Believe it. While you were gone, things changed."

"I know that." He shoved his hands into the pockets of

his jeans. His tone was flat and hard. "That change is exactly what we need to talk about."

The color drained from Kate's face. She closed her eyes and felt almost dizzy. When she opened them, Patrick was watching her intently.

"Who told you?" she asked.

"Shelly. I saw her down at the coffee shop twenty minutes ago."

Kate wrapped her arms around herself and stared out the window on the summer afternoon, then back at him, not knowing what to say.

"When were you going to tell me, Kate?"

"I wasn't."

"What?" He shook his head slowly, as if he couldn't believe what he was hearing. "I am the father, aren't I?"

Kate's temper rose at his implication, but she tamped it down. "Yes, Patrick," she said with a slight snap in her voice. "You are. Technically."

"*Technically?*" he repeated. "You make it sound like I was just a convenient sperm donor."

Kate winced. "That's not what I meant at all."

"Then what did you mean?"

She sighed. "Look. I didn't intend to get pregnant, but I was—I *am*—happy that it happened. I've always wanted to have a child and now I will."

"Great! So what's the problem? We're having a baby. I'm going to be a father. Break out the cigars!"

"No, Patrick. *I'm* having a baby." He opened his mouth, but before he could protest, she continued, "I'm having this baby, and I don't think you should be involved."

"I don't see how I can be any less involved."

"I meant…" Kate paused and took a deep breath. He was making this much harder than she had planned it to be. "My baby *is* going to have a father. But it won't be you."

"It's a little too late to make that choice." Patrick's tone was dry as he raised an eyebrow at her. "I *am* the father."

Kate shook her head. "Not in that way."

"Oh? So who is the father *in that way?*"

"I've got a list of possibilities, but I—"

"A list! And I'm not on it?" With a laugh, he leaned against the workbench again. "What kind of joke is this?"

"It isn't a joke." Kate could feel her face flush, but she kept her chin high. "Face it, Patrick. You would not make a good father. I'm looking elsewhere."

"You can't make a decision like that on your own, Kate. You aren't the only one involved here."

"You're right," she agreed softly. "There's someone else to think of now. I want what's best for the baby. That is not you."

His silver eyes darkened like a storm rolling in from the sea. "You have no idea what kind of father I would be. And you don't have any right to deny me my child."

She squared her shoulders and tilted her chin higher. "Patrick, you're never here. A child needs two parents. *Two.* Are you willing to give up racing so you can be that kind of father?"

"Just because I like to sail doesn't mean I can't be a good father."

"Then you'll give up racing?"

"I don't *have* to give up racing to be—"

"Yes, you do." Kate spoke right over him, ignoring his protest. "This baby needs you here to hold her and love her. She needs you to tuck her in at night, to worry when she's sick, to catch her when she takes her first steps. She needs you *here,* Patrick, not out in the middle of the ocean. Or in some foreign port forgetting she exists."

"I wouldn't forget my own child," he said harshly.

"So you say. But when you race, you seem to forget all kinds of things."

"How do you know anything about it, Kate? You've never even *been* out on a sailboat."

"Whether I know how to sail or not is not the point." Kate was exasperated now, losing control of her temper again. "We're talking about whether you'll be here for this child or not."

He glared at her, but Kate wasn't about to back down. She knew what it was like to have a father who was never around. Her baby would not suffer the same fate. Not if she could prevent it. She would protect her child from that pain, even at the expense of her own heart. Kate turned away from him and felt the heat of the furnace on her face. Usually comforting, this time the blaze fired her anger and unhappiness. She needed to get away from Patrick. If he wouldn't leave, then she would; Kate moved to the door.

Patrick followed and grabbed her by the arm. When she jerked free, he slipped his arms around her. "Please, Kate. Don't run away. It's my baby, too."

She wriggled in his grasp. "You won't be the kind of father a child needs. You won't be here. You're just a sperm donor." She didn't hesitate to use his words against him.

When she tried again to break from his embrace, one of his hands slipped over her abdomen, onto the soft bulge there. Kate stopped struggling. They stood still for a long moment. Kate could feel his breath in her hair and his heart beating against her back.

Slowly, Patrick's other hand slid to her abdomen. He gently cupped the slight swelling where there had once been a flat expanse of skin. Kate didn't stop him. The shield she had erected against him slipped a little as he touched her. This was the father of her child. No matter how she tried to stop it, having him stroke the life they had created brought a lump into her throat.

He spun her around in his arms and raised her shirt. After gazing at her pregnant belly for a long, silent time, his eyes met hers.

"How long?" he asked.

"Four and a half months."

He put a hand on her stomach again, spreading his fingers as if to encompass all that lay beneath the surface. The back of his tanned hand was dark against her pale skin.

"Can you feel anything yet?"

Kate nodded. "She's pretty active. At first it was like having a butterfly trapped inside, but now it's like she's dancing."

"She?" He raised an eyebrow. "It's a girl?"

"I don't know. And I don't *want* to, either, but I don't like saying 'it'."

"I am the father, Kate." He glared at her. "Don't take that away from me."

With a jerk, she pulled back, tugging her shirt down over her stomach. "It's not about what I want or you want. It's about my child."

Patrick locked his eyes on her. "Our child."

"Her happiness is all that matters to me. I don't think you're willing to be that unselfish. I'm not sure you can be."

"You won't even give me a chance, will you?" Patrick thrust a hand through his long hair. He paced away from her across the studio, holding one hand to the nape of his neck. He stood with his back to her for a long minute, then dropped his hand and turned around. "I didn't get you pregnant and then just walk away."

"I know that." Kate took a deep breath. "Look, for me, everything's changed."

"You talk like it's been years. It's only been three months."

"Three months without you. Alone. On my own, with a child to think about. My life is different now, Patrick." She placed a hand over her abdomen where his had rested. "I don't think you're capable of giving me what I need or what a child needs. And, honestly, I can't afford to give you the chance to hurt me again. Or the baby."

"Kate, I—"

"No, Patrick. I'm tired and I don't want to argue about this anymore."

"We need to—"

Kate put up a hand. "No, not today."

He clenched his teeth. "This morning I found out I was going to be a father. Now you tell me I'm not. I need time to think about this. We both do. I'll come back tomorrow."

Kate shook her head. She imagined he wasn't going to let this lie. He was a stubborn man. She also knew that he wouldn't win. The baby trumped every argument he could make. He wouldn't be there as a father for her and nothing less was acceptable.

"Not tomorrow. I have an appointment."

"With who? Your doctor? I'll go with you."

"No." Kate felt a flush creep up her cheeks.

She turned away and began to rack her tools on a Peg-Board panel hung across from the worktable. The loose mandrels clanked together as she gathered them up and put them in a cabinet drawer beneath the board. Carefully, she poured the two dishes of glass frit back into their jars and put them in a rack at the end of the table. She picked up the paintbrush she had dropped earlier and put it in a jar of cleaning fluid. With a rag, she wiped the smear of paint off the table. Patrick watched her closely, but she refused to meet his gaze.

"So you're meeting one of my replacements."

Kate spun to look at him, wide-eyed. "Who told—" She stopped abruptly when she saw his face. He had been guessing, but her reaction had confirmed it.

"You're serious about this, aren't you?" He crossed his arms over his chest. "Damn it, Kate. I can't believe this."

Keeping her flushed face averted, she put away the glass rod he had fidgeted with and screwed the lid on the jar of paint. She swished the brush in the cleaner and dried it with a rag.

"Don't believe it, then, but there's nothing else to say. I've made my decision."

"This is crazy." He stalked to the door and wrenched it open. "This is not over. Not by a long shot." He strode out of the workshop, slamming the door behind him.

Kate jumped at the sound, then plunked herself down on the stool with a sigh. The baby moved restlessly inside her. Soothingly, she stroked the small bulge.

"It's okay, sweetheart. Mama did the right thing." Kate let out a hiccupping sigh as tears ran down her cheeks. "It's over now. It's all over now."

Chapter Two

Patrick skidded his truck into a parking space at the marina, jammed it into neutral and turned off the engine. The gravel lot was nearly empty. Most of the vehicles belonged to marina employees. Their cars were easily distinguished from the boat owners' by age, abuse and layers of dirt. Like Patrick's Dodge: once white, it was now a dull, mottled tan and sported a V-shaped dent in the roof where a mast had accidentally landed on it.

He sat in the pickup, staring out the windshield, hands braced on the steering wheel for a long, silent minute. Then, in a burst of movement, he shouldered his door open, got out and slammed it closed as hard as he could. The truck rocked on its suspension from the force of his fury. Out of the air-conditioned cab, the hot July breeze from the Chesapeake Bay wrapped around him like a wet towel. At the back of the truck, Patrick reached over the tailgate and grabbed his bag of sailing gear.

She can't deny me my own child!

The thought had him dropping the bag and curling his fingers over the warm metal tailgate. *She has no right.* But what could he do about it? With a growl of pure rage, Patrick balled his hand into a fist and slammed it into the tailgate. The blow dented the panel just above the O and shot searing pain from his knuckles up his arm.

"Damn her to hell!"

He spun away from the truck, tucking his hand into his armpit. The action did nothing to soothe the agony. He sat down heavily on the back bumper, still cradling his battered appendage. "Damn her," he repeated softly.

The pain overwhelmed his fury. Slowly, anger was replaced by an ache in his heart that seemed to complement the throbbing in his fingers. That ache was a surprise, a hurt for something he hadn't even known he cared about. He ran his uninjured hand through his hair and lowered his head, hunching his shoulders. His mind reeled and lurched but came up with no direction. Studying the swirling patterns of gravel beneath his feet did nothing to help untangle his thoughts.

"Hey, what's up?" a deep voice asked.

Patrick looked up to see his brother, Ian, standing over him. One black eyebrow was raised in question over his dark brown eyes.

"You don't want to know," Patrick said.

"The reason you just punched your truck?" Ian grinned. He held a canvas tool bag in one hand, a coping saw sticking out one end. The other hand balanced a long oak plank over his shoulder. "Yeah, I want to know." Deftly, he swung the board down and leaned it against the tailgate. He dropped the tool bag in the bed of the truck and took a seat next to Patrick on the bumper. His long legs matched Patrick's as they stretched out from the truck. "Spill it."

Patrick sighed and rubbed a hand over his face. He could think of no way to dress up the truth and make it sound better, so he just blurted it out. "Kate's pregnant."

Ian shook his head and laughed outright. "Well, I suppose it was bound to happen. The Berzanis are a fertile bunch." When Patrick glared at him, Ian shrugged. "So, this is a bad thing?"

"No, it's not a *bad thing*." Patrick ground the words out from between clenched teeth.

"So why attack your truck?"

"Kate doesn't want me involved."

"That's a bad thing." Ian was silent for a moment. "How'd you screw this one up?"

"I didn't screw up!" Patrick rose to his feet to pace. All the anger he had felt came rushing back, pushing aside the hurt. "She thinks I can't be a good father if I'm at sea all the time."

Ian looked at Patrick, his eyes dark and thoughtful. "I see her point. Tough to be good at something if you're not there to do it."

"I could be a good father whether I race or not."

"What, you're going to get the kid a berth in the Trans-Oceana race? Show him the ropes before he can crawl?"

"Of course not."

"Then how are you going be around to do the fathering?"

"Who said I wouldn't be around?"

Ian looked at his hands. "You just did."

Patrick gritted his teeth in frustration. "I wouldn't race all the time. I could cut back some."

"Sounds reasonable. Did you tell her that?"

"She wouldn't let me. She just kept saying she didn't want me involved." His jaw tightened. "She's got a list."

"A list?"

"A list of potential fathers. She doesn't want me, so she's, she's…interviewing other candidates, I guess."

"Really?" Ian was silent again. "What are you going to do about it?"

"Stop her. What else?"

"All right, then." Ian stood and turned to grab his tool

bag out of the truck. Before he picked up the board again, he ran a hand across the dents in the tailgate. "That's number three. How long have you had this rig? Two years? When are you going to stop punching it?"

"Better my truck than your ugly face." With his good hand, Patrick grabbed his own bag.

"As if you'd even have a chance," Ian scoffed, but he smiled at Patrick.

They walked across the parking lot to the marina office, gravel giving way to concrete near the building that housed it. The walkway spread out to the right and joined with the large, open space where the travel lift sat idle. A blue sailboat hung suspended in its canvas slings as Bart, the travel-lift operator, pressure-washed the scum from the hull. Small piles of barnacles, dislodged from the propeller and shaft, lay under the boat. A waft of ripe algae filled the air, borne on the mist from the pressure washer.

At the door to the office, Ian leaned his plank against the wall and held the door for Patrick. "You'd better get some ice on that."

Patrick examined his knuckles, flexing his fingers gingerly. "Doesn't feel like I broke anything this time."

"That's progress," Ian said solemnly, but his eyes twinkled as Patrick laughed.

Cool air-conditioning bathed their faces as they walked inside. Before them was a long, waist-high counter, bare except for a display of brochures at one end, a three-ring binder and a large desktop calendar. The calendar was filled with writing, every date covered, with notes made in the margins, as well. Behind them, against the window, stood two wooden chairs with a low table between them. Supposedly for waiting clients, Patrick could rarely remember anyone actually sitting in the chairs. Most of the people who stepped through the door at A&E Marine were longtime customers who walked behind the counter to grab a cup of coffee from the small break room in back. Or they borrowed some tool. Or they leaned against the counter and talked and talked, sometimes for hours.

Elaine Berzani looked up as they entered the office. She sat at one of two desks behind the counter.

"What have you done this time, Patrick Michael Berzani?" she asked, bustling around the end of the counter and taking his hand. "Ian, go get your brother some ice."

"Ma," Ian protested. "Patty's the one who smacked his truck. Let him get his own ice if he's going to be so stupid."

Elaine leveled a glare at her eldest son. Ian sighed and dropped his tool bag with a clank, disappearing into the break room. Coming back, he thrust an ice-filled towel at Patrick.

"Here, stupid."

"Thanks, ugly."

Elaine frowned at her sons. "Stop it, both of you. Patrick, sit down and keep that ice on your hand. Ian, your father just called and said Jimmy Johnson is down looking at his boat. He'll stall him as long as he can, but you'd better get there right away."

"I told that idiot it wouldn't be done until next week," Ian grumbled, picking up the tools again.

"Don't call your father an idiot." Patrick grinned at Ian and was rewarded with a rude gesture.

"You should be handling Johnson, not me, bro. You're the one who should have test-sailed the damn thing by now."

Elaine rolled her eyes. "Somebody better go. I think the healthiest and sanest one. I'll tend to the injured and insane."

"Tell Dad I'm on my way. You want to go get a beer after?" Ian asked Patrick.

"Yeah. I'll be down on my boat. Tell Jimmy I just got back and I'll take his boat out tomorrow."

Ian nodded and left the office. Elaine went back behind the counter and picked up the walkie-talkie. After she had delivered the message to her husband, she turned and sat down. Her gray eyes surveyed him expectantly. She was a pretty woman, small and sprightly. Dressed in jeans and a powder-pink polo shirt, she looked more like Patrick's older sister than his mother.

Patrick took a chair at the desk that faced hers and propped his feet on the corner. His bruised knuckles felt better—numb from the cold, but better.

"So you punched your poor truck again. What did it do this time?"

"Nothing. I was mad."

Elaine pursed her lips. "That's a news flash. About what?"

Patrick shrugged. "It doesn't matter. I'm over it."

The look on his mother's face told him she didn't believe this fabrication any more than the other lies he had told her. "That's the third time, isn't it?" She shuffled a few papers on her desk. "Or is it four?"

Patrick shrugged. "Ian counted three."

Elaine kept her eyes fastened on him, as if she knew what he was thinking. Patrick said nothing and looked out the window behind her at the docks and the water.

"Well," she finally said. "You haven't told me the other two reasons why you hit your truck, so I shouldn't be surprised that you won't tell me about the third. I'm only your mother. I just brought you into this world. I don't suppose I have any more use in your life."

Patrick grinned. The grin turned into a laugh. "That was good, Ma. Are you giving lessons yet?"

He could see a smile trying to break out on her face, but she wagged a finger at him. "You watch yourself, Patrick Michael."

"But, Ma." Patrick's eyes danced with suppressed

laughter. "I'm only saying that a master at their craft owes it to the next generation to pass that skill along."

Elaine laughed and threw a pencil at him which he caught in his good hand. "Stop it, now." She sobered. "If there's anything you need to talk about, you know I'm here to listen. And tell you what you should do. Like a mother is supposed to do."

"I know that, Ma."

The phone rang and Elaine lifted the receiver. Patrick ignored her conversation, twirling the pencil between his fingers. How could he tell his mother about Kate? Where would he even begin? From the beginning perhaps; he had been sitting in the coffee shop, when his head was turned by a peal of sharp, ringing laughter. It came from a woman at the counter. Running his gaze over her slim, lithe form, he had felt something flicker inside him. Long legs, a sweetly rounded bottom and the taut curve of pert breasts: what wasn't to like about that? Her hair had seemed alive, too, as some stray draft of air caught the long, golden curls and sent them dancing around her head. When she turned and he caught a glimpse of her face and her chocolate-brown eyes, he knew he had to meet her.

Elaine got up, phone in the crook of shoulder and neck and went to a bank of file cabinets along the back wall. How could he tell his *mother* about how hot it had been between him and Kate after that first meeting? That was *not* information to share with a mother. Nor did he want to talk about how suddenly, today, Kate had turned so cold. It cut him to the bone that she could douse the fire so easily, even as she carried his child inside her. The more he thought about it, the more miserable he felt.

Elaine hung up the phone. "All these phone calls! How am I supposed to do any work around here? I never appreciated Tricia until after she'd gone."

Patrick dragged himself out of his muddled thoughts. "What happened to her?" He used the pencil to gesture to the desk where he lounged. "I thought she would have chased me out of her chair by now."

"She moved to Boston two weeks ago."

"Boston?" Patrick gave a shiver. "What would she want to do that for?"

"Love." Elaine smiled at him with a twinkle in her eye. "Isn't that what makes us do all the stupid things we do in life?" She cocked her head to one side, once more looking at her son expectantly.

"I wouldn't know." The words were a mutter as he avoided her eyes. He dropped his feet to the floor, rose, and tossed the pencil back to her desk. "I'm going down to the boat."

"How's your hand?"

Patrick lifted the towel and looked at his knuckles. The skin was blue-white and didn't hurt, but he could see some swelling. "It'll be all right."

"Keep the ice on it." The command was all mother.

He nodded, picked up his bag and swung the door open. "See you later."

"Oh! Before I forget, Jeannie wants you to call her about the picnic on Saturday."

"What does my darling sister need now?" Patrick asked irritably.

Elaine shook her head at Patrick. "Be nice. She needs you to help her with the coolers and ice."

"Isn't that why she has children?"

"It's a *family* picnic, Patrick. That means everyone gets to help."

Patrick rolled his eyes. "I'll call her."

He stepped outside and pulled the door shut behind him. Sighing, he took a deep breath. It was like sucking air through a wet rag—a *hot,* wet rag. It signaled the start of another steamy July in Maryland that would probably last through August. Hoisting his bag on his shoulder, Patrick walked toward the docks that stretched away to the right, past the travel-lift pad.

To his left, three rows of about fifty boats stood on jack stands. Half of those would be gone in a week, to be replaced by others in need of quick repairs or a coat of paint. The other half were serious refits, boats completely stripped of hardware and rigging. Some sported tents of plastic, behind which Patrick could hear the low hiss of an air compressor or the high whine of a gel-coat peeler. The sharp, sweet smell of hot fiberglass mingled with the fecund aroma of the shore. Behind the rows of boats were sheds for the yard's various repair shops: one each for engines, gel coat, paint, canvas and so on. Ian's wood shop was among the largest buildings—big enough to fit an entire boat during the winter. Fragrant with raw wood and varnish, the scent there always reminded Patrick of the childhood he had spent on his parents' old boat.

He went down the ramp connecting the docks to land. The floats bounced slightly with each step and undulated in the wake of passing boats. Like the water they floated on, they rose and fell with the tides of the Chesapeake. Pilings spaced every forty feet or so, driven deep into the mud of Crab Creek, kept the whole maze of docks anchored in place. Patrick passed the small powerboats slipped closest to shore, where the water was shallow. Beyond those were larger, more elaborate yachts, all gleaming fiberglass and bright chrome. Last, in the deepest water, were sailboats.

Patrick turned left onto a narrower dock perpendicular to the main pier. A couple of men, fellow sailors who kept their boats at the marina, greeted him. Otherwise the dock was quiet, as it usually was during the weekdays. It would be busy later; tonight was race night. Patrick flexed his fingers, testing their strength. He winced when two gave him a stab of pain. Maybe he would have to sit this race out.

Ten slips down, Patrick arrived at his boat, *Aphrodite,* a sleek, white sailboat with green canvas over the boom and mainsail. He slung his bag onto the cabin top, then stepped up and over the lifelines onto the deck. The boat rocked gently as he boarded. Patrick adjusted his rhythm to that of the boat and nimbly hopped into the cockpit. There, he pushed open the companionway hatch and pulled out the drop boards to open the cabin.

He went down the steps inside the boat, and threw his bag on the settee that ran along the right side of the boat. The icy, dripping towel went into the galley sink. Moving forward through the cabin, he opened hatches and ports, letting the late-afternoon breeze wash the heat and musty smell out of the boat.

He pulled open the icebox. It held more beer than it had when he left three months ago. He took out one can and, just as he opened it, heard a knock on the hull.

"Ahoy, there, *Aphrodite!*"

With a smile, he grabbed another beer. "Evan, come aboard!"

Evan McKenzie climbed over the lifelines and sat on one of the cockpit seats as Patrick tossed him a can. He popped the tab and took a deep swallow. Patrick climbed out into the cockpit to join him.

Tall, blond and lanky, he looked like Patrick's fair-skinned twin. They had been best friends ever since age twelve when they had tried to beat each other to a pulp over a protest in a sailing dinghy race. After that start, they had gotten into more trouble than seemed possible to their long-suffering parents.

"Welcome back." Evan's greeting was followed by a hearty belch.

"Thanks." Patrick clunked his can against Evan's in a toast. "Thanks for restocking the icebox."

Evan grinned. "Only seemed fair, since I drank what you left in there."

Patrick often thought that his friend looked like a used-car salesman when he smiled like that, sunglasses hiding his green eyes. In fact, he was a car salesman, albeit new ones, and very successful at it. It had something to do with the charm that oozed out of Evan's pores. He could sell a monster pickup to an eighty-year-old grandmother with cataracts or a minivan to a teenager looking for a chick magnet. Patrick didn't understand it. If he didn't know Evan well, he wouldn't trust him on a bet.

"How'd the big race go?" Evan asked.

"You didn't check the site?"

Evan tipped his glasses down to eye Patrick, then pushed them back up. "Please. I've got better things to do with my time than track your wake."

Patrick snorted his disgust. "We took second."

"Against *Voltaic?*" Evan whistled. "Not bad for a bunch of amateurs."

Patrick flipped him off good-naturedly and leaned back against the cockpit coaming.

Evan eyed the swollen, bruised hand. "You get in a fight or something?"

"Punched my truck." Patrick flexed the fingers, again feeling a stab of pain. "Didn't break anything. But I don't think I'll race tonight."

Evan shook his head and slid around to lean his back

against the cabin, stretching his legs out along the seat. "Who pissed you off?"

Patrick saw his brother coming down the dock and didn't answer. Ian climbed on board.

"Ian! You see your brother's knuckles?"

"Yep. That truck will never be the same."

"Any good reason?" Evan cocked his head. "Or just staying in practice?"

Patrick ignored the joke and went below to get his brother a beer. He didn't want to talk about Kate right now. Maybe not ever.

"It has something to do with a woman." Ian took the can Patrick handed him.

"Naturally. Kate?" Evan asked.

Ian nodded. "You'll have to pry the details out of him yourself."

Evan swiveled his head to look at Patrick, one eyebrow raised above the edge of his sunglasses. "She dumped you!"

Patrick sighed. "Look, can we talk about something else?"

Evan and Ian looked at each other, then back at Patrick. "No," they said in stereo.

"He knocked her up," Ian volunteered.

Evan's mouth dropped open and he looked at Patrick over the rim of his sunglasses again. Then he pushed them back up and started to laugh, loud and long. Patrick took a deep drink of his beer, emptying it. He went back down and got another. When he returned, Evan was still laughing, wiping tears from the corners of his eyes. Patrick glared at Ian, who shrugged innocently.

Finally, Evan got control of himself. "Damn, that's perfect," he said on a final gurgle. "Here's to you, Dad," he added, raising his drink.

"That's the tricky part—" Ian began.

"Whose mess is this anyway?" Patrick interrupted.

"Yours, Patty," Ian said. "So, tell him."

Evan looked back and forth between them. "What rest? She's knocked up. You get married, live happily ever after until you don't. End of story."

"That's the problem," Patrick began reluctantly. "She doesn't want to get married—"

"That's perfect!" Evan crowed.

"She doesn't want to get married to me."

"Why not?"

"Kate doesn't think Patrick is father material," Ian said. "He's gone too often racing."

Evan snorted. "What difference does it make if he's here or not? He's the father."

"Tell that to Kate." Patrick popped the tab on his beer and took a long swallow.

"She's going to find a guy who's more qualified for the position," Ian elaborated when Patrick fell silent.

"Wow!" Evan swore. "That's hard-core."

"She wants me to give it up," Patrick added grimly.

"What? Racing?"

Patrick nodded.

"That's ridiculous. You're a world-class skipper!" Evan straightened from his slumped position. "She might as well ask you to stop breathing. What's she got against sailors anyway?"

Patrick shrugged. "Search me. She's never even been sailing."

"Well, you can fix that easily enough." Evan patted *Aphrodite*'s hull.

"So what are you going to do?" Ian asked.

"Somehow, I have to change her mind. I have to show her that I can be a good father."

"Hey, I know! Just borrow one of Jeannie's kids for a few days to cart around with you. Kate'll get the idea." Evan chortled at his own joke.

"Knock it off, Evan." Patrick glared at his friend. "I'm serious."

"Oh, come on. It's not like she has guys lined up to marry her," Evan scoffed. "She's *pregnant*."

"She has at least one," Patrick countered. "She's meeting him tomorrow."

Evan shook his head and took another swig of beer. "I don't believe it."

"I do," Ian said quietly.

Evan looked at him.

Ian shrugged. "She's beautiful and vivacious. She's an artist. Smart, too. And she runs her own business. The fact that she's pregnant wouldn't be that much of a deterrent for some guys."

"It would be for *me*."

"No one's asking you to step up to the plate, McKenzie," Patrick said.

"Sounds like no one's asking you to, either, Berzani," he shot back.

"Shut up, both of you," Ian interjected. "So, how are you going to change her mind, Patty?"

"Go see her tomorrow, before she meets this other guy. If I can talk to her, I think I can make her see it could work."

Ian nodded while Evan shook his head. "It's going to take more than fancy talk."

"Maybe I should take your advice, then," Patrick said slowly.

"*My* advice?" Evan asked, surprised.

"Yeah." Patrick nodded as he thought through the idea. "I should take her sailing. She'll understand everything then."

Evan grinned. "Brilliant!"

"I don't think that's such a good idea, Patty," Ian said, frowning. "She's never sailed and—"

"That's why I should do it," Patrick interrupted. "I'll surprise her and show her how great it really is."

"But what if she hates it?" Ian asked.

"Never happen," Evan said. "I'll go along to do the work and Patrick can play skipper."

"I am a skipper," Patrick said drily.

"Yeah, yeah. Whatever."

"Guys, I *really* don't think you should do this." Ian looked back and forth between them. His dark eyes were worried. "At least don't spring it on her."

"No, Patrick's right," Evan said. "It works better if he surprises her. She'll love it!"

Patrick ignored his brother and Evan. He wasn't sure how he felt about becoming a father, but he wasn't going to let Kate push him aside before he figured it out. He had to change her mind. Taking her sailing was the perfect first step. Perfect.

Chapter Three

Kate carried her cup of tea out onto the brick patio behind her house. The early-morning air was cool and fresh after the heat and humidity of the previous day. Later, it would be hot, but now the temperature was perfect. She sat on a deck chair and looked at the garden.

Peeking out from behind the daisies, peonies and petunias were fantastical ceramic creatures sprung from Molly's fertile imagination. Some of the beasts sported smooth, shining skin in ocher, sienna and russet. Their eyes glinted slyly. Others were rough-hewn and mossy, features grumpy and fierce. Between them, shining spires of red, green, blue and yellow glass—creations from Kate's studio—spiked skyward. Delicate orbs of lustrous silver and gold glass hung from the branches of the wisteria, catching the light and reflecting it back to the house.

At the edge of the patio stood several large ceramic pots, also Molly's handiwork. Crimson geraniums spilled over their sides, spicing the air with scent. Kate took a sip of her tea and savored the morning air. She emptied her mind, trying to concentrate on the whimsical beauty of the garden, but it was no use. All too soon, the pansies and marigolds were overlaid by Patrick Berzani's angry face. She closed her eyes and sighed.

As the baby fluttered in her stomach, Kate went over the previous afternoon in her mind. *Again.* Her argument with Patrick was all she could think about, worry about. The night had been filled with disturbing dreams about him. In one, she and Patrick had soared through the air like eagles. They each held the hand of a tiny baby that squealed and giggled. Kate had felt exhilarated and free. When she turned to her companion, his face had changed, and her brother Danny looked back at her through large, sorrow-filled eyes. The baby's hand slipped from her grasp and the two figures dropped away from her, falling through the air, becoming smaller and smaller. Kate had tried to scream but couldn't. She woke with a gasp, her heart pounding. After that, she had given up on sleep and dreams and risen to make tea, hoping a new day would put the old one behind her.

"Good morning."

Kate opened her eyes and looked up to see a tall woman in a bright orange-and-gold caftan step onto the patio. Her wild hair was caught up in a messy bun on the back of her head, tendrils flying and dancing as she moved.

"Molly! Good morning. When did you get back?"

"Late last night. I should still be sleeping, but the morning's too glorious to miss." The older woman brought her mug to the table and sat across from Kate with a sigh of satisfaction.

"How did the festival go?"

"Amazing," Molly said, excitement lighting her oval, tanned face. "I sold everything! There wasn't a cup or a vase left at the end."

"Fantastic. I'm glad it went so well."

"Me, too. It was definitely worth the trip." Molly studied her carefully. "You look tired."

"I didn't sleep well."

"You'll have to get a nap in later." Concern shone in the pale blue eyes looking at Kate.

"That's my plan."

"Good." With a nod, Molly leaned back in her chair and stretched like a cat, slow and long. She closed her eyes and raised her face to the sun, smiling happily. "Oh, what a *wonderful* morning."

Kate smiled as she watched Molly. She knew her aunt wouldn't care one iota that the sun highlighted every line on her face. She had told Kate often enough that she didn't understand women who fought time. There were too many other interesting things to do with life than trying to look young. She was a woman comfortable with herself and her age.

With her hair, her wild caftans and a love for bright lipstick, Molly was the stereotype of an artist. She lived alone, happy and content by herself, in the house next to Kate's. A common wall joined the two residences and they shared the garden with separate patios on either end. Behind the houses, fronting the main street was the retail shop they also shared. On the other side of the alley was the studio with Kate's furnace and Molly's kiln.

Their work complemented each other's perfectly. Their shop, FireWorks, was popular and profitable enough. Molly claimed that Kate's fantastic glasswork was the reason. The pieces had an airiness and delicacy that tempted the eye. Kate returned the flattery, pointing out how much of Molly's colorful, fanciful pottery flew out the door every day. They had been in partnership for five years, ever since Kate had finished school and her apprenticeship.

It was through Molly that Kate had found her passion. As a girl, she had been fascinated by the clay and minerals her aunt used to create pottery. Shaping the raw materials and burning them into a new, solid form intrigued her. With Molly's encouragement, Kate took it one step further and discovered molten minerals—glass—and her true artistic calling.

Kate ran her finger along the rim of her tea mug. Bright green with stripes of blue, pink, purple and orange, it was one of Molly's bolder designs. She didn't want to spoil the tranquility of the morning, but she had to talk to her aunt, the one friend in whom she could confide.

"Patrick's back."

Molly's eyes snapped open. "You saw him! How did it go?"

"Not so well. He knows I'm pregnant."

"You told him?" Molly asked in surprise.

"No, Shelly did. She told me she thought he knew. Oh, Molly," Kate groaned, covering her face with her hands. "I made such a mess of it all. When he asked about the baby, I just panicked. Then I lost my temper."

Molly chuckled. "I'm sure it wasn't that bad."

"It was bad enough." Kate sighed. "I should have been cool and firm. I've already made the decision, right? All I have to do is stick with it."

"Does he know what you've decided?"

"He does now," Kate said ruefully. "Poor Patrick."

Molly snorted. "*Poor Patrick,* my fanny. He deserves whatever he gets. He's the one who disappeared without a word."

Kate sipped her tea. "I suppose so. I can't help wishing I'd handled it better, though."

Who would have guessed that she, even tempered to a fault, could be so moody? When she got weepy during a commercial for laundry fabric softener, she had known something was wrong. A trip to the doctor had confirmed her suspicions. She had cried, then laughed. More than once since, Kate had found herself laughing and crying at the same moment. The abrupt mood swings embarrassed her, but she had no control over them. She sighed again, regretting yet another emotional outburst.

Molly leaned forward, her elbows on the table. "Did seeing him change your mind?"

"No. Nothing's changed." Kate looked at her aunt and shrugged. "He gave no excuse for not keeping in touch, just that he was busy with the race. He said he was sorry, but that doesn't mean much." She paused, then added in a whisper, "He forgot about me. What if he forgets his own child, too?"

Tears swam in Kate's eye as she said the words aloud. It hurt right down to her soul to experience that indifference again. She thought she was over the pain but apparently not. Being abandoned by someone you loved was something you never got over.

Molly reached out and took Kate's hands in hers, squeezing them tightly. "You know what the future is like with Patrick Berzani. If you want a different childhood for this baby than you and Danny had, then *you* need to take charge and make it happen."

"I know I do," Kate said, feeling comfort in her aunt's warm handclasp. "But am I nuts, Molly?"

"Wanting a good father for your child?"

Kate nodded, looking at Molly hesitantly. "At least, going about it the way I am seems crazy to *me* sometimes," she admitted.

Molly looked at her intently. "Well, as I've said before, it's a bit out of the ordinary, but I wouldn't call it crazy. And you could raise the baby on your own. I'll be here to help." She cocked her head to the side. "But then I will be anyway, regardless of what happens."

Kate felt a lump rise in her throat seeing the support

and love in her aunt's eyes. "What would I do without you?"

"Probably get along just fine." Molly released her hands and sat back.

"I doubt that." Kate sipped her tea, silent for a minute. "You know, you're part of the reason I want a family for this baby," she said, stroking a hand across the slight mound of her stomach.

"Me? Why do I get the blame?"

Kate smiled at the astonishment on Molly's face. "Because you've been the best aunt in the world, and the best friend. You've been more of a mother to me than my own."

"Isabelle never had a maternal bone in her body. That's not your fault, Kate. She has your father and that's her life. End of story."

"I know. I stopped expecting her to act like a mother a long time ago." Kate shifted in her chair. "But you've given me a taste of what a real family could be like. I want more aunts like you. And uncles, brothers, sisters, everything. For me and my baby." Leaning forward, Kate set her tea to one side. "I want a family, Molly. A *real,* honest-to-goodness family, with squabbles and fights and holidays and vacations all jumbled up together."

"You want what you never had."

"Yes, I suppose so," Kate said with a nod. She rested her elbows on the table. "That's why Patrick won't do. What's the point of building a family with a man who's never going to be around? Or who would forget us as soon as he left the house?"

She and Molly shared a sad smile, then her aunt chuckled. "Besides, it would never work out. He loves water and you're deathly afraid of it."

"True."

"Does he know that yet?"

"No. I couldn't tell him. How do you tell a man who loves the sea that every time you get near water more than three feet deep, all you can think about is drowning?"

"He'd probably understand if you told him about your first and only swimming lesson," Molly said. "Not everyone's father begins by tossing their five-year-old into the deep end of the pool."

"It wasn't quite that bad." Kate shook her head. "It doesn't matter what story I tell Patrick anyway."

"True enough." Molly picked up her mug. "So what's on your schedule today? Are you working in the studio?"

"Maybe later. I'm going to tackle some designs here at the house this morning, then I have lunch with Steve Craig."

"Bachelor number one." Molly laughed.

"I wish you'd stop calling him that." Kate frowned as she sipped her tea.

Molly was unrepentant. "I can't help it. I don't think your scheme is crazy, but it *is* funny. It's so like you—creative but excessively well planned."

"Well, it's planned up to a point. I'll see what Steve thinks about my crazy idea before I start patting myself on the back."

"The worst he can say is no, right? Then it's on to bachelor number two." With that, Molly rose from the table. "I'm going over to the studio for a while. Is Shelly in the shop today?"

"Yes, she'll open up at noon."

"Good. I'll give her a call later and let her know I'm around if she needs help." Molly sauntered off the patio toward the studio.

Kate took her empty mug into the house to begin her day. Just how the day would go, she had no idea. It depended on Steve's reaction to her proposal.

She had known Steve Craig for two years. They had gone out a few times when they first met, but there had never been a spark for Kate. Steve still called her once in a while, but she had always evaded his invitations for dinner or a movie. Now, since she wasn't looking for herself, she evaluated him in a different light.

Steve was gentle and kind. He had patience and humor, two more important qualities for raising a child. He was stable, too, owned a house not far from hers and had lived in town for more years than she had. She couldn't pick someone more likely to be there for her baby. He owned his own plumbing contracting business with ten employees and a reputation for quality work. Today, she would find out if he was interested in the additional job of becoming a father.

After a cool shower, Kate pulled a sundress out of the closet. The yellow print was cheerful and bright, in contrast to her glum mood. She wound her long hair into a twist and anchored it against the back of her head with a gold clip. Wispy tendrils immediately worked their way out to tickle her cheeks and the back of her neck.

In consideration of the afternoon heat, Kate put on a minimum of makeup. She smoothed on tinted sunscreen, followed by a little eyeliner to bring out the gold in her brown eyes, mascara and lip gloss. Grabbing her white sandals, she left her bedroom to get her sketch pad from the living room. As she walked down the hall, the doorbell sounded. Who could that be? It was too early for Steve. She pulled open the door and wished she had checked the peephole first.

"Good morning." Patrick smiled at her.

Startled, Kate was at a loss for words. She reminded herself that she was not giving in to this attraction. She must be strong.

"Good morning. What are you doing here?"

Patrick leaned a shoulder against the door frame, close enough for her to be surrounded by the aroma of his after-shave. The crisp lemon scent reminded her of other mornings after he had spent the night with her. His beard was heavy, so he usually rose early and shaved, then came back to bed. To her.

His cheeks would be soft and— Kate gritted her teeth, forcing the memory away. That didn't matter now.

"I thought we could take a drive this morning." Patrick was solemn. "To talk."

Kate shook her head. "I don't think so."

"Come on, Katie." He took her hand. "We do need to talk about this more. You know that."

She shook her head again, but he squeezed her fingers lightly. "Please, Kate."

The quiet entreaty swayed her as a demand could not have done. She remembered again how badly she had handled yesterday. Patrick was right. They did need to talk. He had to see the truth; the best thing he could do for the baby was recognize that he was not the right man for the job and step aside. It wouldn't make him a bad person. Just the opposite; it would show that he really did have the best interests of their baby at heart.

"Let me get my purse."

Patrick waited on the porch until she returned, then led the way to his truck. He opened the door for her and helped her inside. It struck Kate how thoughtful he was in these small, gentlemanly ways, but so *thoughtless* in other, larger ones.

"I've been thinking about what you said yesterday," Patrick said, once they were out of her driveway and headed down the road. "About me not being around for you and the baby because I race. I would be here, Kate."

"All the time?"

"As much as I can. I could cut back on the racing."

"But you still plan to race," she said quietly.

Patrick's jaw clenched, but his voice was even when he spoke. "Yes, I still plan to race."

"Then you'd better turn the truck around." Kate's tone was flat and hard.

"Wait a minute. I thought the problem was that I was gone so much of the time. Now you're telling me I can't race at *all?*" Patrick spoke slowly. "What is this, some kind of test for fatherhood? How many other qualifications are you going to throw in?"

"It's not a test."

"What is it then?" He looked over at her briefly, his eyes cool.

Kate shifted uncomfortably in her seat. "What happens when you're out racing, Patrick?"

"What do you mean?" He frowned, confusion in his tone. "What has this got to do with—"

"On that last race, your boat almost sank."

"No, it didn't." Patrick shot her a glance. "Are you talking about the knockdown?" He snorted, shaking his head. "They kept calling it a broach, but it wasn't even close. The mast didn't touch the water."

"Patrick, I saw the footage. The boat looked like it was going to go completely over."

"I was *there,* Kate. We were fine."

"They said you were taking too many risks with the boat. You were pushing too hard. You should have been more careful."

"Careful doesn't put you in the winners circle," Patrick said stiffly. "That's what it's all about. Those guys weren't out there. They didn't know the conditions. I did."

"But they said you had too much sail up. That you *always* have—"

The truck jerked to an abrupt stop at a red light and Patrick turned to face her. His eyes were intense, his jaw set. "The commentators second-guess everything, Kate. That's their job. If you kept listening, you would have heard them say that my tactics brought us from the back of the fleet to second place. If I'd had a day longer, I'd have *won* that race."

Kate stared back at Patrick. She bit her lip, not wanting to continue the argument but unable to stop herself. "It sounded like you pushed too hard." She paused. "Like that day last February."

A car horn sounded behind them. The light had turned green and Patrick put the truck in motion. "That was different," he said, keeping his eyes on the road.

Was it so different, Kate wondered, *or just more of the same?* She turned her face to look out the side window, remembering the cold, brilliantly clear winter day. The fierce wind had seemed to light a spark in Patrick's eyes. He and his team were match racing another boat across the Chesapeake, from Baltimore to Rock Hall. She dropped him off at a marina in the Inner Harbor and drove around to meet the boat on the other side of the Bay.

Waiting for him at the dock, she heard Patrick's voice on the VHF radio in the marina office. The dockmaster had turned up the volume to follow the race's progress. Patrick and another man argued about how close he was sailing to a container ship. The man—the ship's pilot—told Patrick to change course. Patrick refused. "Don't worry about it," he said. "I'll clear you."

"Change course *now,* Captain. I have the right-of-way in the shipping channel."

"Actually, I have the right-of-way, since I'm under sail, but I don't have time to argue about it," Patrick's voice had crackled back. "Maintain your course and let me worry about mine."

With that, Patrick had signed off and Kate waited, tense until she saw his boat round the breakwater. She rushed out of the office and down to the dock in time to see the Coast Guard also pull alongside the pier. The Coast Guard officer had been coldly furious with Patrick and berated him for jeopardizing the safety of his crew. Patrick claimed that he knew exactly what he was doing; there was no risk. The officer said it was reckless and threatened to revoke his license. Finally, Patrick apologized. That hadn't been the end of it, though. "I'm not wrong," he had muttered after the Coast Guard officer walked away. "And I won the race."

Kate had felt her stomach sink. He was so certain that he was right, that the risks he took were not risks at all. Every day that she followed his race across the Atlantic Ocean, she had the same feeling inside. It grew agonizingly stronger when the boat had nearly capsized. Patrick Berzani lived on the edge and he liked it just fine out there.

Patrick turned the truck left at a stop sign and Kate saw that they were heading down to the water.

"Where are you taking me?" she asked.

"I need to check on a boat. Do you mind?"

"I thought we were going for a ride." It was just like Patrick to plan one thing, then change his mind midstream.

"We are. This is just a slight detour." Patrick turned off the road and into a gravel parking lot.

"What marina is this?"

"It belongs to my parents," he said, pulling into a parking spot next to another car. "You've never been here, have you? I was going to bring you once."

"That was in March. It was too cold, blowing like crazy and raining sideways."

"Today's the perfect day then. Come with me. You have

to see this boat." Patrick opened the door and jumped out of the truck.

"I'd rather wait here."

"Come on, Kate." He coaxed her with a smile. "It's too hot to stay in the truck."

Kate couldn't think of a reason to say no, not without revealing her fears. Boats of any kind made her nervous. It wasn't the boats that worried her, really. It was all the water around them. She had successfully avoided getting on one with Patrick so far, but her luck had apparently run out.

When he got out of the truck and came around to her side, she slid out and let him take her hand to lead her to the docks. Down the ramp, Kate could feel the slight give of the wood surface as it absorbed their steps. She swallowed. Her hand involuntarily tightened on Patrick's. He looked over and smiled at her, curling his fingers around hers. She couldn't even bring herself to pull away, as she knew she ought to. His hand was a lifeline she wasn't willing to let go.

Kate nearly laughed aloud as they walked farther and farther out over the water. *Of course,* she thought, *the boat would be all the way at the end of the dock.* She had feared she would freeze in terror when she was out on the pier, with the water all around, but she surprised herself. It wasn't so bad. The floats moved a bit underfoot, but they felt stable, not likely to suddenly tilt and dump her in the creek.

Without Patrick pointing it out to her, Kate knew immediately which sailboat he meant to show her. She knew next to nothing about boats, but she knew fast when she saw it. This one was sleek and low to the water. Its blue hull reflected the ripples around it and the new stainless steel fittings sparkled in the sun. *Blue Magic* was emblazoned across the stern. The wood railings gleamed, layered with a golden varnish as smooth as freshly blown Pyrex.

Patrick toed his shoes off on the dock beside the boat, swung aboard and turned to extend his hand to Kate. She took a step back. There was no way she was getting on that thing, no matter how nice it looked.

"Come aboard. I'll give you a tour."

"No, thanks," Kate said, shaking her head. "I can see it from here."

"Jump on, Kate," Patrick urged. "This boat is amazing. It's a Hainesworth. You have to see it to believe it."

"I can believe it just fine from here."

"Come on. It's a rich man's toy. They don't make many like her."

Kate struggled for a minute before letting curiosity take over. She did wonder what a boat like this would look like inside. From the outside, it was a beautiful, sleek machine. As long as it stayed tied to the dock, she would be fine.

She slipped off her sandals, reached out and took Patrick's hand. As she stepped aboard, the boat gave slightly, though not much more than the docks had. Once she was on deck, Patrick released her and Kate felt a moment of panic. She watched him walk to the cockpit with casual grace. She set her jaw. *I can do this,* she told herself. *It's safe. Perfectly safe.*

Moving cautiously, holding her hands out for balance, Kate followed Patrick's path. The boat felt solid, and though it sloped toward the water, the bare teak deck under her feet was rough enough to keep her from slipping. Kate found natural handholds, too: a wire, a rope, a railing on top of the cabin. When she reached the cockpit, Patrick took her hand again as she stepped down into it.

"You made it," he teased with a grin.

Kate merely smiled back nervously. "I'm walking for two now, you know."

"Welcome aboard." He bowed with a flourish and kissed her hand. "To both of you."

They stood on a wooden grate inset into the floor of the open cockpit. Behind her was a large wheel on a white pedestal. On either side, seats stretched the length of the well, topped with navy-and-cream-striped cushions.

"Wow. Very nice."

"Wait until you see below." Patrick pushed open a sliding hatch opposite the wheel and lifted another hatch board out of the entrance down to the cabin. "The companionway stairs are steep, so turn around and treat them like a ladder."

Kate followed his instructions and cautiously made her way down the steps. She was glad she was barefoot. The wood was varnished and felt slippery, even with the ridges carved into each step for traction. Once down below, she turned around and gasped. "It's so short."

Patrick laughed, his hands resting on his knees as he bent over in the low-ceilinged cabin. "It's a day-sailer. No one's expected to spend too much time down here."

She looked around. Despite the low headroom, the boat looked like someone's living room—a very wealthy, very short, someone's living room. Everywhere she looked, varnished teak gleamed golden warmth. Matching sofas ran along either side of the cabin. The cushions were covered in pale cream leather, plump and inviting. Behind the settees were built-in cabinets, each with a louvered door and gold-plated knob. Patrick flipped a switch on a panel next to the steps and recessed lighting brought the interior to life.

"Some toy," Kate murmured.

Patrick chuckled. "It's only used for afternoons on the Bay, maybe evening sails. If you go somewhere overnight, you get a hotel. Though it has a cozy V-berth in the bow."

"But it's such a big boat."

"Forty-two feet of glorious perfection." At her look of incredulity, he shrugged. "Fitzgerald was right. The rich are different than you and I."

"Different meaning they're crazier."

"Something like that. I know the owner. He's a good guy. He's just got more money than sense."

"So what are you doing with it?"

"It's new and he wants all the systems checked over before he takes her out."

Kate frowned. "But, if it's new, shouldn't it be ready to go?"

Patrick snorted. "That'll be the day. A boat like this usually has a fathom-long punch list of things that don't work. And that's better than most. I've seen some boats that practically had to be rebuilt after they left the factory."

"So you test things, sail it, then fix what's wrong?"

Patrick nodded. "Let's go up topside." He gestured her to precede him, and turned the lights off.

Once back in the sunshine, Kate slipped on her sunglasses. Patrick joined her and sat down on the bench in the cockpit. He seemed in no hurry to leave.

"Don't you need to do something here?"

"I did it when we first went down below. I checked the hydraulic fluid, made sure it wasn't leaking."

"So, we can go?"

"Or we can talk here. It's a nice morning for enjoying the water."

Kate sighed and sat opposite him. Nestled in the protection of the comfortable cockpit, she felt less afraid of the water all around her. She opened her mouth to speak and the boat shifted, startling her.

"Hey, Patty," Ian said as he stepped onto the cushion beside Kate and sat down next to her. "And hello, Kate," he added, dropping a kiss on her cheek.

Kate smiled at Ian, happy to see him. She had liked him from the moment Patrick had introduced them. The brothers were vastly different—Ian reserved where Patrick was gregarious—and they balanced each other out. Patrick always surging ahead, Ian, more cautious and thoughtful, keeping him in check. It was a pleasure to be with these men who were friends as much as brothers.

"What are you doing here?" Patrick seemed surprised by the intrusion.

"I thought you might need a hand," Ian said. "Unless you've changed your mind. Not that it's ever happened before."

"If it's a good idea, why change it?" Patrick asked. He sounded annoyed.

Ian cocked his head as he looked at his brother. "Because your track record stinks?"

"Don't you have some chunk of wood that needs to be cut or drilled?"

"I think I can be more useful here."

Kate looked back and forth between the two men. She felt as if she were at a tennis match, but she didn't know who was ahead. "Is something wrong?"

"Not yet," Ian said with a shrug and stood up.

The boat shifted again. Kate turned to see Evan McKenzie climb aboard. She was less than happy to see him. As much as she liked Ian, she and Evan were like sandpaper and silk: they could rub each other threadbare. Evan was almost like Patrick, but with some key ingredients missing that left him too arrogant, cocky and sometimes just rude.

"About time you showed up," Patrick said by way of a greeting.

"I had to close a deal. This guy wanted to buy a Hummer," Evan countered with a sly grin. "Who am I to refuse his money? Hey, Kate," he greeted her. His tone was polite but cool. "Ready for the fun?"

Kate smiled slightly. "What *fun* would that be?"

"Ah, that's the surprise." Evan went forward on the boat and began pulling lines at the mast.

"Just sit tight and I'll explain in a minute," Patrick said.

"But, what—"

Before she could complete her sentence, Ian stepped out of the cockpit, avoiding her eyes as he went. Patrick disappeared down below. When he climbed back up into the cockpit, he slid behind the wheel, opening a small door built into the side of the boat. Kate was surprised to see a panel of buttons and instruments appear from what looked like a solid piece of wood. He fiddled with the instruments for a second and Kate felt a faint vibration. A hiss and splash of water sounded at the stern of the boat. She felt an instant of worry that quickly grew to fear.

"Ready when you are," Patrick called to Ian and Evan.

To Kate's horror, she saw the two men untie the lines holding the boat to the dock. Ian took a long pole and pushed the bow away from the pilings. Patrick manipulated a chrome handle on the wheel pedestal and Kate found herself in a boat leaving the safety of land.

"What are you doing?" She kept a tight rein on her fear and tried to pretend that they had not actually left the dock. "The boat's not tested yet, is it?"

"You're going to love this," Patrick said, grinning widely. His eyes were on the water around them as he maneuvered the boat.

"Love what?" Kate gulped down her terror. "Patrick, I want to go back to the dock."

"Hoist the mains'l," Patrick called to Evan, then turned to her. "It's a gorgeous day on the Chesapeake. I said I'd take you sailing sometime and I thought today would be the perfect day."

As he spoke, a large sail rose over Kate's head. The brilliant white cloth fluttered and flapped in the wind. Kate's hands were white-knuckled, clinging to the edge of her seat. The shore was getting farther away. It was all she could do to keep herself from screaming.

"Patrick! We have to go back. Please, turn this boat around."

At the same time the sail went up, the boat entered open water. Ian came back to the cockpit, yanked on a rope and the sail at the front of the boat—whatever it was called—unrolled like a window shade pulled out sideways. Evan dropped into the cockpit and pulled on yet another rope on the cabintop.

The boat was skating over the waves now. Patrick pushed the chrome handle again, then leaned over to push another button. The faint vibration she had felt disappeared as did the instrument panel. He had turned the engine off, she realized. Kate swallowed hard. She tried not to look around. She was on a boat completely surrounded by water.

Deep water.

She turned. Land already seemed very far away. The boat not only looked fast and felt fast, it *was* fast. Evan pulled on a smaller rope at the front of the cockpit and Ian started turning a crank on one of the big chrome drums across the cockpit from where she sat.

"Round her up, skipper," Evan called back to Patrick. "Let's see what this baby can do!"

At his words, Patrick spun the wheel over. Ian kept cranking, while Evan grabbed the end of the rope and pulled. Wind whipped across the sails and through Kate's hair, sending tendrils flying around her head wildly. The bow plunged into a wave and seemed to almost bury itself into the water. Then salt spray flew back into Kate's face. If she had thought they were going fast before, they were flying now. She braced herself and squeezed her eyes shut. The wind seemed to catch the boat and pick it up, tipping it over.

And over.

And *over*.

She opened her eyes and saw water. She was looking *down* at the water. The boat was about to tip all the way over. Too late to tell Patrick that she couldn't swim. She was going to die. Her baby, too. Terror bubbled up and over. She couldn't control it any longer. Tears welled in her eyes and spilled over as her fingers bit deeply into the fabric of the cushions. In total, mindless panic, she screamed.

Chapter Four

The moment Kate shrieked in terror, Patrick sprang into action. "Ian, take the helm!"

Ian lunged and grabbed the wheel as Patrick dove for Kate. He snatched her into his arms and pressed her to him, feeling the frenetic beat of her heart. Pulling away slightly to see her face, he removed her sunglasses. Her paper-white skin, dilated pupils, and the tears streaming down her cheeks made the bottom drop out of his stomach. He pulled her tightly against him once more.

"Katie, what's wrong? Is it the baby?"

She was shaking like a leaf, clinging to him like a limpet. He felt her fingernails pierce his skin through his shirt.

Evan knelt beside them. "What's wrong?"

"I don't know." Kate still had her face buried in Patrick's neck. He tried to pull her away slightly, so he could see her face again, but she wouldn't let go. "Please, sweetheart, tell me what's wrong."

"We're going to drown." Kate was crying into his shoulder.

"What?" Patrick didn't think he had heard her right. "What do you mean?"

"The boat's going to tip over." Her words came out in staccato between gulping sobs.

A light dawned in Patrick's head. His own fear subsided. "No, it won't, Katie." He ran a hand over her back, trying to soothe her. "It's supposed to tip like this. We're perfectly safe."

"Especially with a scream that loud." Evan snorted a laugh, shaking his head. "The Coast Guard station in Baltimore must have already heard it and sent out a rescue boat."

"Shut up, will you, McKenzie." Patrick glared at Evan. This was not the time for smart remarks. He pulled Kate tighter to him.

Evan rolled his eyes. "Relax, Kate," he said impatiently. "This is great sailing. Enjoy it."

Kate shuddered again as the wind gusted and the sailboat heeled over a bit farther. Patrick felt more tears soak his shirt.

"Make it stop!" she moaned.

"Katie, I—"

"I'll drown if we tip over, Patrick." Kate finally lifted her head so he could see her face. Her brown eyes shone nearly black with panic. "Please don't let my baby die."

"We're not tipping over and you're not going to drown, I promise you." He kissed her mouth and cheek. "Trust *me*. You and the baby are safe."

The boat shivered in the wind and she dove into the shelter of his arms again. "I can't swim," she wailed.

Patrick realized there was nothing he could say that would calm her. She was too frightened to understand that the boat was designed to sail on a heel. He looked over at Evan, still kneeling next to them.

"Drop the sails."

"What? We just got out here. The wind's—"

"Drop them," Patrick ordered. "We're going back."

"But—"

"Bring her up into the wind," Patrick called out to his brother. "We're going to drop the sails, turn on the engine and go back."

"Is Kate okay?" Ian asked.

"She's scared when the boat tips. She's afraid of the water. If we head back under power, she'll be fine."

Ian immediately turned the boat and brought it dead into the wind. Evan pulled on the furler lines for the jib and it rolled up into a neat cylinder on the head-stay. Minutes later, he had the mains'l rolled into the boom and stowed. Patrick held Kate in his arms, stroking her back and murmuring soothing things into her ear. As soon as the boat leveled out, he felt a slight easing in her grip. The tremors that shook her subsided to random shivers.

He ignored Ian and Evan at first, concentrating on Kate. Then his brother caught his attention. Ian worked the throttle lever with one hand while pushing the start button with the other. From the look on his face, Patrick knew there was trouble.

What's wrong? He mouthed the question.

Ian shrugged. "Engine turns over fine, but won't start."

Kate raised her head. "We're stuck out here?" Her voice carried a note of renewed panic.

Patrick swore to himself, then forced a smile to his face as he looked down at her. He dropped a kiss to her cheek and smoothed a hand over her hair again. "It's all right, sweetheart. Don't worry, we'll get it fixed." He turned to Ian. "Stub said there was an air bubble in the fuel line the other day that he had to bleed. He said he fixed it when they changed the filters, but maybe there's a leak somewhere."

Ian nodded and went below. Patrick turned to Evan. "Can you take the helm?"

"Sure, for all the good it will do." Evan looked over the side. "We're pretty much dead in the water."

"Dead!" Kate's voice rose in alarm.

"Don't worry, Kate." Patrick glared at Evan. "We're safe. We'll get this fixed and get underway."

Evan sat behind the wheel and acted like he was steering the boat. They both knew there was nothing much he could do without propulsion. They were adrift, but Patrick didn't want Kate to know it. She needed all the illusion of safety they could give her.

He turned to the woman he held in his arms. She was still pale, but she wasn't crying anymore. "How are you doing?" He kept his voice soft as he captured her eyes with his own, trying to convey confident, calm serenity. Anything to ease her fear.

Kate swallowed and looked away. "Not so good. I can't help—"

"I know you can't." Patrick stopped her words with a kiss. "I wouldn't have brought you out here if I'd known you would be so frightened. Why didn't you tell me?"

"When did I have the chance?" she snapped.

Patrick almost smiled at that. That was more like the Kate he knew. "Well, any time over the past hour." He thought for a second. "Or back in February when we first met?"

"We were away from the dock before I could say anything," Kate answered. "You told me you would just look at the boat, then we'd leave. Then you *surprise* me with this!" Her voice rose with each word until she was nearly shouting. Fury had replaced fear.

Ian stuck his head out of the companionway at that moment. He quickly shook his head at Patrick. "No go. We're going to have to sail her in."

Patrick closed his eyes for a moment. *What a mess.* He could check the engine himself, but even if he found something that Ian had overlooked, they had few tools or spares with them to do repairs. He opened his eyes. There was no use hiding reality from her any longer.

"We have to sail back, Katie."

"It won't be like it was before," Ian added. "We'll be going downwind, so the boat won't tip so much."

Kate looked at Ian, her eyes pleading. "Really?"

Ian nodded and patted her shoulder. "We'll take it slow," he said with a smile. He stood on one of the cockpit benches and surveyed the water around them. "And there's not so much wind now. We'd better get going." He shot a glance at Patrick.

Patrick read what his brother was thinking in a second. He saw Evan scan the water, too, and wince. The wind *was* dying. Fast. A typical July day on the Chesapeake. They needed to get going before it died out altogether.

Frustrated, Patrick watched as the other two men did all the work. He couldn't let go of Kate. Or, rather, she wouldn't let go of him. The idea of sailing—of tipping over—had her clinging to him again. The sails went up in a matter of minutes. The wind was now a mere breeze, but it was blowing the right direction. Evan took the helm.

Their slow passage through the water toward land eased Kate's fears. She let loose her tight grip on Patrick's arms and sat back a little. Ian offered her a handkerchief so she could wipe away her tears and blow her nose.

"Thank you," she said. "I must be a mess."

"I've seen worse," Ian answered with a smile. "You should have been there when we got hit by a gale off Patagonia. Patty got doused by a wave when he went up to drop the jib. He swallowed at least two gallons of seawater. He looked like a drowned cat, and spent the next hour with his head over the side." Ian chuckled. "*That* was worse."

Kate managed a short laugh. "I guess it would be."

"You should have filmed that," Evan said.

Ian shook his head. "Too rough for the camera, but it would've been good footage."

"Yeah, so you could embarrass me," Patrick added acerbically.

"Of course," Ian agreed. "Anything to keep you in your place."

The three men laughed, then fell silent.

"It seems dangerous," Kate finally said.

"What does?" Patrick asked.

"Sailing."

"Not really. It has its thrilling moments, but it's not that dangerous."

"But the boat almost tipped over," Kate protested. "And that boat you raced *did* go over on its side."

"That was a different situation," Patrick said. "What happened today was normal. It's called heeling. The wind pushes the sails, but the weight in the bottom of the keel pushes back." She looked skeptical and he brushed a finger over her cheek. "I can explain the aerodynamics of a sail and how that transfers power to the keel, if you want."

She shook her head. "I'll pass right now."

"Sailing's only dangerous when you forget to be careful," Ian said.

"That's right," Evan piped up. "Remember Benny Stillson last season? The boat jibes, the boom hits him in the head and he's dead like that." He finished with a snap of his fingers.

Kate's eyes widened and she gulped.

"Do you have to tell that story now?" Patrick ground out.

"It's not a story," Evan shot back. "It's fact. And there are lots of other instances like that one."

"He was a good sailor. I never understood how he missed that call," Ian said.

"One too many beers, is my guess," Evan answered.

"Benny didn't drink."

Evan shrugged. "Who knows? It was an accident then. Happens to the best of them."

Patrick could see the horror on Kate's face as she listened to the exchange.

"That's right," he said. "It was an *accident*. They happen all the time, even on boats."

"Yeah, they do, so you can't say sailing isn't dangerous," Evan argued.

"I didn't say it wasn't dangerous."

"Yes, you did." The protest was made in triplicate.

"I *said*, it's not *that* dangerous." Patrick was annoyed that his brother and best friend were hurting his case with Kate. "How many people die in car accidents every day?" Patrick looked at Kate as he spoke. "Accidents happen whether you're on land or at sea. You walk across the street and get hit by a car. Or some idiot crosses the line on a narrow road and there's a head-on collision. Or you slip in the bathroom and crack your head on the tub. Is walking across the street dangerous? Is driving dangerous? Taking a bath? No, of course not. Sometimes accidents just happen."

"But you expose yourself to unnecessary dangers on the ocean," Kate said. "And what if you fall off the boat? Or get hit by the boom, like Evan said? A thousand miles from nowhere, there's no one to help you." She paused, searching his eyes. "And you *choose* to be out there."

"Things like that rarely happen, Kate. We're harnessed in, tethered to the boat, and there's a full crew to help anyone who is injured. You should worry more about me when I get in my truck and drive to the grocery store. Or when I walk down the stairs at your house."

"But you're less likely to die in one of those accidents than you are on a boat on the ocean."

"That's not true," Patrick said in frustration. "What do I—"

"Ahoy, there, *Blue Magic!*"

The crew all looked over to starboard. A small power-boat pulled up alongside and Ian jumped up to grab its rail. A skinny runt of a man stood grinning at them.

"Youse all look like you might be wantin' a tow."

"Yeah, Stub," Ian said. "That would be nice, since it's your fault we're stuck out here."

"My fault! How's that?"

"The fuel line is fouled and we couldn't get the engine started."

"Well, you the fools taking out a boat when I ain't finished workin' on her engine yet. Course, I thought I got 'er all cleared." Stub scratched his head. "I guess I'll have to take another peek. Toss me a line, Ian."

Ian and Evan scrambled to get the sails down and some towlines rigged. Patrick shifted Kate to one side and lifted the cushion to get into the locker beneath their seat. He pulled out three fat white fenders and passed them to Ian. Once they were secure alongside the launch, Stub put the engine in gear and guided them back to the marina.

Kate was silent on the return trip. Patrick watched her closely, but she refused to meet his eyes. She seemed calm, but her fingers were wound together tightly. Stub maneuvered them into the dock carefully. All three men jumped off and secured the boat in her slip. With a wave, their rescuer left them, shouting that he would look at the engine later that day.

"Hey, they're calling for winds up to twenty knots on Thursday," Evan said. "You want to try this again?"

"Get lost, McKenzie," Patrick snarled at him.

"What'd I say?" Evan was the picture of wounded in-nocence, his green eyes wide and guileless.

"What didn't you say?" Patrick began then, checking to see that Kate could not overhear, whispered, "Would it have killed you to help me out a little?"

"What do you mean?"

"He's pissed because you told Kate about Benny," Ian said.

"So?"

"So, she's terrified out of her mind and you tell her about some guy dying on a sailboat," Patrick hissed. "How big of an idiot are you?"

"Well, it's the truth. I—"

"I'd like to go home, Patrick," Kate said quietly.

Patrick spun around to see her standing on the side-deck right behind them. She held out a hand that he ignored. Instead, he reached up and grasped her by the waist, gently lifting her down to the dock. He held her steady as she slipped into her sandals, then put on his own shoes.

"I'll see you guys around," she said to Ian and Evan.

"You feel better?" Ian asked.

She smiled. "I will once I get to shore."

Patrick walked with her up the dock and to his truck. He helped her inside, went around the hood and got in the cab.

"Kate. I—"

"Skip the explanations, Patrick. Just take me home."

He hesitated, then stuck the key in the ignition. They made the journey back to her house in complete silence. Kate kept her head turned away from him, looking out the side window the entire way. At her house, he pulled into the driveway and turned off the engine.

"Don't get out," Kate said. "I'll see myself inside."

"I'm sorry, Kate."

She shrugged. "I know. Me, too. It's over, so let's just move on, okay?"

She turned away and slid out, closing the door with a firm thud. Patrick watched her walk around the hood of the truck. She didn't look at him once and he felt like banging his head on the steering wheel in aggravation. It had been a disastrous morning. Now they were back to square one or somewhere worse. He got out and followed her. He couldn't just let it end like this. She was halfway up the steps when he caught up to her.

"I really am sorry for what happened. Can we just talk about this, please?"

She turned and looked at him, her eyes dark and enigmatic, before continuing up to the front door. "I don't think there's anything to say."

Patrick moved and took her arm gently, preventing her from inserting her key into the lock. "If I had known you would be so frightened, I would never have taken you out there."

"I *know* that, Patrick. You don't have to keep apologizing. I'm as much to blame for what happened as you are. I should have told you I was afraid of the water."

"Then why won't you talk to me?"

"Because there isn't anything else to say," she repeated.

"Of course there is. We have to talk about the baby, Kate. I want to be a part of its life, of *your* life. I think we can make it work between us." His voice trailed off as he watched incredulity spread across her face.

"You really are something, Patrick Berzani. You *still* think that, after this morning, there's hope for you and me? Well, guess what? I'm thinking just the opposite. Today, you demonstrated precisely why I want you far away from me and this child."

"What did I—"

"What made you think taking me for a sail was a good idea? Especially without any warning?"

"I thought if I could show you how good it was out there—"

"You told me you wanted to *talk,* Patrick. Not sail."

"I wanted to talk. Honest!"

"I suppose we were going to have a nice chat, just the four of us? You, me, Evan and Ian? You're hopeless."

"I didn't know you were going to freak out."

"That's not the point!" She was shouting so loud, the whole neighborhood could probably hear. "The point is that you risked my life out there and the life of our child!"

"I didn't!"

"You didn't ask me if I could swim. Or give me a life jacket. Or even tell me where one was," she said, ticking off points on her fingers. "Does that sound like good father material to you? I'm *four-and-a-half months pregnant,* Patrick. What if I'd gone in the water?"

Patrick ran a hand through his hair and walked to the edge of the porch. He turned back and looked at Kate. With her hair waving softly around her head, her face flushed with anger and her eyes bright, she looked beautiful. If only she wasn't so stubborn. If only all his plans for the morning hadn't gone so wrong.

"So where do we go from here?"

A car drew up in the alley next to the studio, drawing Kate's attention. Her eyes flickered over his shoulder, then back to his face. Patrick couldn't read her expression, she had closed herself to him completely.

"I don't see how we can go anywhere."

He opened his mouth to dispute her words, but was interrupted by the man who had gotten out of the car.

"Kate! Hello."

Patrick turned to look at the tall, barrel-chested man coming up the walk. He had a round, cheerful face with a wide smile and bright blue eyes. Those eyes glanced at

Patrick for a second, then returned to Kate. He climbed the steps of the porch and took her hands in his, kissing her on both cheeks. Patrick's fists clenched.

"You look gorgeous," the man said.

"Hello, Steve," Kate said with a slight smile. "Are you early or am I late?"

"I'm a bit early," the man admitted. "I couldn't wait to see you."

Kate unlocked the front door, then glanced at Patrick. "Thanks for stopping by, Patrick."

"Aren't you going to introduce us?" Patrick asked.

Halfway through the door, Kate turned around, obviously reluctant. "Steve, this is Patrick Berzani. Patrick, Steve Craig."

"Pleased to meet you." Steve shook Patrick's hand.

"Let me guess. You're one of my replacements."

Steve looked puzzled. "Replacements? What do you mean?"

"Leave it alone." Kate glared at Patrick, but he ignored her.

"Congratulations. You're Kate's first choice," he told Steve.

"Well, that's good news," Steve said jovially. "I've been working on her for two years."

"It's taken you that long?" Patrick raised an eyebrow.

"Just leave," Kate said. She took a position between the two men, facing Patrick.

He looked over the top of her head at Steve. "I'm really honored to meet you. It takes a heck of guy to volunteer to raise another man's child."

"Kate, what's he talking about?"

"You mean she hasn't told you?" Patrick asked.

"Shut up, Patrick," Kate said stonily.

"*What* is going on here?" Steve asked.

"Well, you see, Steve, Kate's pregnant." Patrick smiled disarmingly at his rival. "I'm the father, at least biologically, but since I'm not quite up to her standards, you've been selected to take my place."

Patrick watched with satisfaction as Steve's eyes widened and his mouth opened and closed several times like a fish gasping for air. Kate flushed bright red.

"Of course, I don't intend to just disappear. I'll be hanging around, keeping an eye on things in case—"

"That's enough." Kate's arms were folded tightly across her chest as she scowled at Patrick.

"I suppose you're right. I'd better be going. You two have a lot to talk about." Patrick smiled slightly as he brushed a finger over Kate's cheek and nodded at the other man. "Nice meeting you, Steve."

He turned on his heel and walked back to his truck. As he got in and drove off, anger once more burned a hole in his heart. She might think that it was over, but it wasn't. Not now and not ever.

Chapter Five

With her safety goggles strapped in place, Kate scooped up a glob of molten glass from the crucible with the end of a blowpipe. She kept the pipe turning as she placed the ball onto the flat steel marver and rolled it into an oblong shape. The glass glowed a bright orange as she worked, losing color slowly as the heat dissipated. When it was smooth, she rested the pipe on a floor yoke, thrusting the glass-covered end of it back into the oven. Rollers on the tall, Y-shaped stand kept the pipe rotating and balanced the weight of the glass. Even through the dark goggles, she had to squint as she stared into the glowing flames of the oven.

A swell of strings from the stereo followed the choreography of her work. The baby kicked in time to the music, as if demanding to be a part of the creative process. Kate laughed and patted the small life inside her. From the first, the baby had been most active whenever Kate worked in the studio. She wondered if her child would be a dancer, since she moved to the music so much. The baby fluttered again, a one-two punch against her stomach. *Either a dancer or a soccer player.*

When the glass was hot again, she pulled the yoke back and blew a series of staccato puffs into the pipe, watching as the oblong expanded. One hand in a Kevlar mitt cupped the globe to control the shape as she blew and spun. She could just see the pattern of irregular spots where specks of metal were suspended in the walls of the vessel. In the hot, glowing glass, only her imagination could see what the final colors would be: deep red and gold flecked with silver strands. She took off the mitt and put the globe back into the oven until it was a white-hot blaze, then pushed the glass down into a sand mold. The mold formed the bottom of the piece and gave it a sharp, jagged base to contrast against the smooth sides of the bowl. She used a hand-torch to keep the neck hot and blew more air into the pipe, expanding the globe.

As she worked, Patrick was never very far from her mind. Steve pulled a close second. Though she hadn't seen either man for two days, she was still angry. And hurt. Kate felt a flush climb her cheeks that had nothing to do with the temperature in the studio. How *dare* Patrick stick his nose in something that wasn't his business. Why couldn't he understand that it was over between them?

When the globe reached the size she wanted, she allowed it to cool slightly, and then used a wooden mallet to break away the mold. With a dollop of hot glass, she attached a punty to the newly exposed base. She scored the neck with a jack and broke the blowpipe free with a tap of a mallet. Deftly, with smooth turns of her wrist, she kept the shape rolling and turning, this time with the punty.

She wasn't any happier with Steve. After Patrick's bombshell, her so-called suitor couldn't get away fast enough. The whole fiasco with Patrick and Steve had shaken her resolve about finding a father for her child. Maybe she should just raise the baby alone. Then she wouldn't have to deal with the male half of the species at all. Kate's lips tightened. More heat from the torch kept the glass pliable as she worked to expand the mouth of the globe and used a wood paddle to flatten the rim.

Her mind still on Patrick, Kate grabbed another small glob of glass, spun it out and traced it around the lip of the opening, creating a smooth bead. She rested the punty on the floor yoke and put the orb back into the oven for more heat. When she judged it hot enough, she pulled it out and twirled it sharply. The bulbous globe abruptly became a bowl. Swinging the punty as she twirled, she added a decorative wave around the lip and finished the piece.

Molly walked in just as Kate brought the bowl upright. "You're just in time. Give me a hand for a second, will you?"

Molly grabbed a set of Kevlar mitts off the rack. When she had the bowl cupped in her hands, Kate tapped it off the punty and opened the annealer. Molly set it inside, where it would cool for a few days, the heat slowly dissipating until the glass hardened. Kate shut the door.

"That was gorgeous," Molly said. "I've never seen you do anything like that before."

"It's a new process using a sand mold."

"I hope there's more where that came from."

"I don't," Kate said sharply. "Given who inspired it."

"Patrick? Is that why you're worked up?" Molly asked with a sympathetic smile. She slipped off the gloves and wiped her brow. "Patience, dear. It will all work out."

Kate tucked a strand of hair back into her bandanna. "I hope you're right, but just now I'm losing hope."

Her aunt gave her a hug. "You'll get your family, Kate. You just have to keep working at it."

"Thanks."

"I've got to go get a load of clay," Molly said. "Do you need me to run any errands for you?"

"No, but thanks for the pep talk."

"That's my job," Molly said with a chuckle.

Molly left the studio and Kate pulled out another blowpipe. She started forming a small glass vase and continued mulling over her situation. When she finished the piece, she looked at it critically and started another. Four hours later, she placed a third vase alongside the first two and the bowl. Kate closed the door to the annealing oven. She ought to be happy; for the first time in days, she had finished four pieces that pleased her. The bowl might even turn out to be one of her best works yet. Her aggravations had finally fueled her art instead of interfering with it.

Kate turned off the lights and closed the door behind her with a snick of the lock. Outside, she breathed in the summer air, which, despite the heat, felt cool to her after hours in front of her furnaces. She could smell the spicy scent of geraniums from the garden, a welcome change from the acrid odor of hot dichroic. Pulling off her bandanna, Kate ran her fingers through her hair to let the breeze lift and separate the long damp strands. Walking leisurely along the path to the house, she spied a visitor seated on her steps. He rose when he saw her.

"What are you doing here?" Her question was blurted out without thought.

"Why, hello, Kate," Evan McKenzie said. His eyes were hidden by sunglasses, which gave him the appearance of an enforcer. "It's a pleasure to see you, too."

Kate flushed with embarrassment at his pointed pleasantness; her question *had* sounded rude. "Hello, Evan," she said, keeping her tone neutral this time. "What can I do for you?"

He stuck his hands in his trouser pockets. "I'm here because of Patrick."

"Oh? Is it any of your business?" Kate moved around him and up the steps.

He stopped her with a hand on her arm, pulling off his sunglasses to hold her gaze with his own. "He's my friend. I'm making it my business."

Kate saw the determination in his face and sighed. "All right. Come inside then."

Evan followed her into the house, down the hall to the kitchen. He took a seat at the table while Kate pulled a pitcher of iced tea out of the refrigerator. She filled two glasses, gave one to Evan and sat down across from him. After drinking deep of the icy liquid, she set the half-empty glass on the table and looked at him expectantly. He fidgeted with his own glass, but didn't take a sip. She ran a finger over the condensation that had formed on the side of her glass. The room was quiet except for the faint tick of the clock on the wall. Now that he was here, Evan seemed to have nothing to say.

Finally, he spoke. "Kate. About Patrick—"

"Did he send you?"

Evan looked surprised at her question. "Me?" he asked, then laughed once. "I'm the last person Patrick would send as an emissary." His cool green eyes warmed as he laughed a second time in genuine amusement.

"Then why are you here?"

"Because he's been my best friend for nearly twenty years. I know him."

"That's nice but—"

"He's very sorry about what happened on the boat."

"I know. I accepted his apology already."

"He still feels at fault."

Kate rubbed a hand across her forehead. "Look, I know you're here to help Patrick, but this really is just between him and me."

Evan's gaze sharpened, but his voice remained smooth. "Then why not make an effort to work things out with him?"

Kate took a sip of tea. "He's not cut out to be a father."

Evan snorted. "Come on, Kate. Who really <u>knows</u> what kind of parent they'll be before they've got a kid to practice on?"

Kate opened her mouth to speak, but Evan beat her to it. "You haven't seen all sides of Patrick. He's great with kids. Have you ever seen him around his family?"

"No. I've only seen him with Ian."

Evan leaned forward and shoved the glass of tea to one side. He clasped his fingers together and surveyed her coolly. "What if I told you that family was one of the most important things in Patrick's life?"

"I wouldn't believe you."

"What if I could prove it to you? Would you give me a chance to do that?"

Kate was uncertain what she should—or could— answer. "I'm sure Patrick loves his family, but that doesn't have anything to do with him and me."

"Sure it does," he said softly, his eyes intense. "This is about building a family, isn't it? And whether Patrick's qualified for the job. But you're dismissing him before you've done a thorough background investigation."

Kate squirmed in her seat. "So how are you going to prove to me that I'm wrong?"

"Tomorrow. One o'clock at Bayside Park. Be there."

"Why?"

"Patrick's parents are having a picnic for the marina crew and the family."

"I really don't think this is going to make a difference, Evan."

"I think you're wrong." Evan paused. His eyes were

fierce, boring into hers. "But don't take my word for it. Come see for yourself. You owe him that much, Kate. He may not be perfect, but he's a good guy."

"I never said he wasn't."

"No?" Evan stood, pulled his sunglasses out of his shirt pocket and slipped them on, hiding his eyes again. "But you made him think it, which is pretty much the same in my book."

"I don't want to hurt him, but I have to think of this baby."

"Then do it for the baby. Come to the picnic because you owe it to your child to see what Patrick is really like when he's with his family."

She couldn't read him at all now, not with the sunglasses masking his face. She was reluctantly impressed with his defense of Patrick. She hadn't thought Evan capable of a serious conversation like this.

"Okay, Evan. I'll see if you're right. I'll come to the picnic."

"Good. I'll see you tomorrow." His mission accomplished, Evan turned to go. Kate followed him through the house and out the front door. On the porch, he looked back at her.

"You're a good friend, Evan."

"He's family. I would do anything for him."

"I believe you mean that."

"I do." Evan tipped his sunglasses down, letting her see how serious he was.

"One more thing."

"What's that?"

"Remind me to never buy a car from you."

"Haven't lost a sale yet," he said with a grin and a wink.

With that, Evan McKenzie turned and walked down the

sidewalk to where a sleek red convertible waited. He got in and drove away with a single parting wave. Kate watched him go, silently chewing over his words. She couldn't believe he had talked her into going to the picnic. As she went back inside and closed the door behind her, she muttered, "What have I done now?"

KATE PULLED HER CAR into a parking space and turned off the ignition. Signs posted at the entrance to the park had directed her this far. Sounds of laughing, screaming children would lead her the rest of the way. She could hear them even with the windows rolled up. Kate made no move to join them. The car started to warm in the sun, but still she sat. She was sure that if she got out of the car and joined the picnic, she would be committing herself to something. What, she wasn't sure. But surely, just attending a picnic didn't mean she had changed her mind about Patrick. A hot dog and potato salad were not going to miraculously make him a better father. So why not start the car and drive away?

Because you owe it to Patrick. You owe it to your baby.

Kate grimaced. The voice of her conscience sounded remarkably like Evan McKenzie's. The thought was enough to goad her into moving. She grabbed her purse and slid out of the car, letting the joyful sound of children lead her toward the festivities.

She walked over the hot asphalt, then onto grass and under trees, where she felt immediately cooler. Across the lawn, a large pavilion was filled with picnic tables, a barbecue and people. Smoke drifted up and over the crowd as they set food on the tables. A red, green and white banner strung between posts announced the "Annual A&E Marine Picnic." Balloons and streamers decorated the rest of the pavilion, waving gently in the breeze.

A Frisbee landed at Kate's feet, startling her. She reached down to pick it up just as Evan came jogging over.

"Kate. What took you so long? I was beginning to think you'd chickened out." He held his hand out for the disc.

"Smart-ass," she said tartly.

Evan grinned. "And that's one of my lovable traits."

"Does Patrick know I'm going to be here?"

Turning abruptly away, he shouted across the lawn. "Hey, Patrick! You've got a guest!" Then he turned back to Kate. "He does now." Evan threw the Frisbee to a young boy and ran off.

Kate saw Patrick spin around at Evan's shout. He was standing under the wide branches of a tall maple, an older woman with bright red hair by his side. The shout drew everyone's attention to Kate. She tried to ignore the stares and kept her eyes on Patrick as he walked toward her.

"Hello, Kate. What a surprise." His greeting was friendly enough, but she could see the suspicion in his body, the way he walked, the stiff set of his shoulders. "What are you doing here?"

Kate lifted her chin. "I got a special invitation. From Evan."

Patrick slid his sunglasses to the top of his head. His eyes were opaque, but his brows rose, signaling his surprise. "Really? What'd he have to do to drag you here?"

She shrugged. "I can leave if you want."

Patrick stared at her for a long moment. "What about Steve? Does he know you're here?"

The question caught her off guard, making her reply harsh. "I don't think that's any of your business."

"Yes, it is," Patrick said in a low tone. "Everything about this is my—"

"Patrick, dear. Why don't you introduce me to your friend?"

The red-haired woman had come up beside him without either of them noticing. She examined Kate with the same clear gray eyes as Patrick's, but hers were bright with curiosity and a touch of humor.

"Ma, please—"

"I'm Elaine Berzani." The woman held out a hand, grasping Kate's with birdlike bones. "Patrick's mother."

"Kate Stevens."

"I'm so glad to finally meet you," Elaine said cheerfully.

"It's nice to meet you, too," Kate replied.

"Patrick didn't mention that he had invited anyone."

"I hope I'm not intruding."

"Oh, gracious, no. The more the merrier."

"Give us a minute, will you, Ma?" Patrick asked. "Kate and I need to talk."

"Nonsense. What you need is a nice plate of barbecued chicken." Elaine ignored her son's scowl and slipped an arm through Kate's. "Come along, dear. You look hungry."

"Mrs. Berzani, I—"

"Please, call me Elaine." She patted Kate's arm. "We can't have my newest grandchild starving to death, can we, dear?"

Kate turned to look at Patrick, shocked speechless by Elaine's words.

"Who told you?" he asked.

"Ian did. The day you hit your truck." Elaine looked surprised. "Am I not supposed to know? Is it a secret?"

Patrick ran a hand through his hair in obvious bewilderment.

"Well, it won't be one for long now, will it?" Elaine patted Kate's stomach affectionately. "Pregnancies never are," she added with a laugh.

"Mrs. Berzani, I—"

"*Elaine,* Kate. Please, I insist." The older woman beamed a smile at her. "I can't tell you how pleased I was to hear about the baby. Of course, it would have been better to hear it from the source—" she shot a look at Patrick "—but no matter. What *does* matter is that you are here today."

All at once the small woman enfolded Kate in a warm embrace. The unexpectedness and the sincerity undid her. Tears welled up in Kate's eyes and a sob slipped out from her throat. She closed her eyes against more tears.

Elaine's grip tightened and she rubbed a comforting hand over Kate's back. "There, there, dear. Having a baby's a roller-coaster ride, isn't it?"

The understanding words broke the dam inside Kate. She started to cry in earnest, great, gasping sobs of sorrow, happiness, anger and joy all jumbled together. She had no control. All she could do was hold on and wait for the end. Kate felt hands grasp her, drawing her away from Elaine. Seconds later she was clasped in Patrick's strong arms. The fit was so much better, his shoulder at the perfect height for her head, his grip the exact pressure she needed to feel secure.

Slowly, her sobs subsided. Kate kept her face turned into Patrick's neck. She could hear the steady thud of his heart in her ear and felt her own heartbeat slow to match it. His hand stroked her back, soothing her from nape to waist. Another more delicate hand patted her gently, too. A napkin was slipped into her hand and Kate grasped it blindly.

"Oh, no," she moaned.

"It's all right, Katie," Patrick said softly in her ear.

She lifted her head and saw the large damp spot on Patrick's gray T-shirt. She blotted it with the napkin until Patrick grabbed her hand.

"Don't worry about it." She looked up to see him smiling tenderly down at her. "A little salt water hasn't hurt me yet."

"I'm sorry," she whispered. "It's just that your mother was so nice. I didn't expect it."

Patrick pressed a kiss to her lips. "No, I'm sorry." He squeezed her gently. "This is my fault."

"No, I—"

"Sometimes I forget you're pregnant," he interrupted. "My sister, Jeannie, cries all the time when she's expecting. We take turns seeing how little a thing will set her off," he said with a glint of mischief in his eyes.

"And Charlie is ready to scalp you all by the end of the first trimester," Elaine added with a slap at her son's arm.

Patrick merely grinned. Kate turned to face Elaine, slipping away from Patrick. He only let her go so far, keeping an arm around her waist.

"I'm sorry, Mrs. Berzani. I don't usually cry all over people I've just met."

With a soft touch, Elaine grasped Kate's hands in hers. "I knew there was something bothering my son. I'm glad you're it. Now, Patrick, bring Kate along for some food," she added with one last squeeze of her fingers. "Antonio will be just as thrilled to meet you."

Kate found herself in the midst of the crowd of people under the pavilion. Patrick stayed at her side, introducing her to first one, then another person. The names went in one ear and out the other. Someone pressed a bottle of beer into her hands. Patrick whisked it away and called for a can of soda. He kept the beer for himself, took a long drink, then dropped a kiss on her lips. Kate blushed and pulled away.

The can of soda arrived, carried by Ian. He grinned at her and offered her a damp cloth, too. "Ma said you might want this, Kate."

"Give me that," Patrick said, taking the cloth. "Hold this." He handed her his beer and ran the damp fabric gently over her cheeks.

"Let me do that, Patrick." Kate reached for his hand, but he dodged her grasp. "I should go clean up. I must be a mess."

"You look fine, Katie." He pressed a kiss to her lips again and several women giggled.

Elaine arrived at their sides, looking at the couple with a proud smile. "A little water never hurt anyone. Besides, we're going swimming later. We'll all look just as water-logged then."

"I think Kate and I will pass on the swimming. We've had too much fun around the water lately," Patrick said. He tossed the cloth away and took his beer back from her. "Let's get something to eat."

Taking her arm, he drew her through the crowd to the barbecue. A tall man with dark hair turning silver presided over the smoking grill. He had on an apron that read I'd Rather Be Sailing, and a red baseball cap cocked back on his head at an angle. Kate immediately knew she was looking at Patrick's father.

"Pop, this is Kate." Patrick pulled her in front of him. "Kate, this is my father, Antonio Berzani."

"How do you do?" Kate said, holding out her hand.

Antonio dropped his spatula on a plate. "Ellie! Is this the one?" he shouted to his wife. At her nod, he reached out and took Kate in a hug, lifting her from her feet before setting her gently back down. He held her at arm's length, beaming a huge grin at her. He put a large hand on her belly, a gesture so like Patrick's that Kate felt tears sting.

"Welcome to the family," he said gruffly. "Both of you, welcome."

He pulled Patrick into his arms then, hugging him with

bluff blows to his back. "Patricio, you've done good," he added, kissing him on both cheeks.

Kate felt the situation spin out of her control. "Oh, but—"

"We need to feed her, Ellie," Antonio said. Elaine had come to stand at his side. "Give me a plate."

Kate's eyes widened as she saw two pieces of chicken, three sausages and a hamburger loaded onto the large paper plate and shoved into her hands.

"Get her some potato salad, Patricio," Antonio instructed. "And some lasagna. Don't forget the corn, either!"

Patrick steered her through the crowd to a table filled with dishes. "Don't worry," he said, taking another plate and filling it with various salads and savory treats. "I'm eating half of this. Just don't let Pop know you didn't finish it all by yourself."

"Patrick, we do need to talk," Kate said as he led her to a table near the side of the pavilion, under the spreading branches of a tall tree.

"Eat first, then talk. That's the Berzani rules."

"But they think we're together."

"Aren't we?" Patrick took a drink of his beer, then laid a napkin on her lap and handed her a fork.

"No," Kate said seriously. "We're not."

"Because of Steve?"

"I don't think he matters."

Patrick ate a bite of chicken. "Why not?"

"He doesn't…" She looked away across the park. "Apparently, I overestimated my own appeal."

Patrick gave a snort of derision. "He's a fool."

He broke a roll apart, buttered it and handed her half. The simple gesture touched her. She took the roll and bit into the softness. The flavor piqued her appetite. She picked up her fork and joined Patrick in demolishing the heap of food on the two plates. A third dish, filled with three more types of salad and two ears of corn, slid onto the table in front of them.

"Pop sent this over," Ian said as he joined them at the table. His own plate was filled to monumental proportions.

"Keep eating like that and you'll get fat," Patrick said, pointing at the pile of food.

"Hasn't happened so far." Ian shrugged, eyeing them closely. "You two finished fighting for the day?"

Kate and Patrick exchanged a quick glance. "We weren't fighting," Patrick denied.

"Only because Ma intervened." He took a bite of baked beans. "You're the talk of the party."

Kate flushed and Patrick frowned. "Back off, Ian."

A short, pretty woman with red hair just like Elaine's joined them at the table. "Can't you guys go one minute without snapping at each other?"

"Of course we can," Ian said. "What's our personal best, Patty?"

"I don't know." Patrick put his fork down to make an exaggerated count on his fingers. "Maybe five, six minutes?"

Kate laughed.

The woman smiled at her. "I'm Jeannie McGuire. Older sister to these two idiots."

"Kate Stevens."

"So, what'd Patty do to make you cry?"

"Jeez, Jeannie," Patrick protested. "Why do you always blame me?"

"Why wouldn't I?" Jeannie's large blue eyes were innocent. "She shows up, you walk over and she's crying. Be warned," she confided to Kate. "He's an awful tease. I recommend you ignore him as much as you can."

Patrick laughed. "If only you'd follow your own advice."

Jeannie shot him a glare, then turned back to Kate. "As bad as he is now, he was worse when we were kids."

"Remember on that J-boat Pop had, when you thought he'd drowned?" Ian asked.

"Oh! That was awful!" Jeannie put a hand to her chest. Her eyes were round with remembered horror. "When we were kids," she said to Kate. "We were out sailing on this little boat and Patrick pretended to get hit with the boom. He goes overboard and disappears. I completely freaked out. Ian's looking over the side and I'm screaming at him."

"I saw Patty catch the boom when we turned and dive off the boat," Ian added. "He popped up right away, but Jeannie missed it. She's screaming like a banshee and Patty gives me the signal to keep my mouth shut."

"I kept looking over the side of the boat on one side, and Patrick would swim to the other," Jeannie said.

"It was so funny." Ian took a sip of his beer. "Jeannie was streaming snot and I'm *dying*, trying not to laugh."

"It was awful!" Jeannie aimed a smack at Ian's arm. He ducked and laughed again. "You were *terrible.*"

"It *was* funny." Patrick joined them in enjoying the memory. "She wouldn't speak to us for days."

"I got you back, though, didn't I?" Jeannie said, her eyes narrowed. "With the shaving cream."

Patrick chuckled. "You did at that."

"Mom!" A boy of about seven ran over and tugged at Jeannie's sleeve. "Dougie pushed me down."

"What did you do to Dougie first?" Jeannie asked.

"Nothing!"

"Hmm, really?"

The boy squirmed but defended his innocence. "Really! I didn't do nothing."

"Anything."

"Exactly," the boy agreed. "We were just playing soccer and Dougie kept hogging the ball—"

"Meaning he was winning, so you decided to even the odds," Patrick interrupted.

Jeannie held up a hand to stop the protest that was tumbling out of her son's mouth. "Go back and apologize to Dougie for trying to cheat."

"Mo-*om!*"

"*Now,* Charles Alan. Or you can sit here with us adults until you learn to play the game by the rules."

Jeannie eyed her son sternly and he huffed a sigh of defeat. With a soft smile she pulled him to her and pressed a kiss to his forehead. "I know it's a drag being youngest, but cheating isn't going to help anything."

With another dramatic sigh, the boy turned and ponderously walked away toward the other kids playing soccer. Jeannie shook her head and turned back to the table.

"Just wait. In a few years you, too, will have this kind of fun."

Obviously, their "secret" was no such thing here. Kate shifted uncomfortably, and felt like a fraud. The Berzanis were all so welcoming to her. Even Patrick seemed certain of the future. And there was something different about him, surrounded by his family. Kate hated to think that Evan might be right; seeing him with them did make a difference. Or was she imagining it? Maybe she just felt envious that he had the family she had always wanted.

"Maybe we'll have a girl," Patrick said to his sister. "She'll be just like Kate."

"I hope you have ten boys all *exactly* like you," Jeannie said. "Sorry, Kate. I wouldn't wish that on you, but on Patrick?" She paused, then shot her brother an evil grin. "Oh *yeah.*"

"Because he was so awful to you as a child?" Kate asked.

"To me and everyone else!"

"Come on! I wasn't that bad," Patrick protested.

Ian chuckled. "Yeah, you were. I think Mom started to get gray hairs the minute you were born."

Kate looked over at Patrick. "Just what did you do, besides tormenting your sister?"

"Nothing. I was a good little Boy Scout."

"Hardly," Jeannie said. "If you can think of any trouble a kid could get into, Patrick got into it. I thank my lucky stars my two boys don't have *half* the imagination and foolhardiness that Patty had as a kid."

"He was the worst daredevil," Ian told Kate. "He built a hang glider out of two-by-twos and an old spinnaker and launched himself off the roof of the metal shop at the yard. The thing went down like a stone," he added with a laugh. "Patty's lying there, broken pieces of wood sticking up all around him and Ma thinks he's dead."

Kate looked at Patrick, eyes wide. "Were you hurt?"

"A few scratches. Nothing broken."

"*That* time," Jeannie interjected, then went on to relate another incident where Patrick had not been so lucky.

Kate laughed as Patrick's siblings related the childhood exploits of the man sitting next to her. Slowly, as daring deed piled on top of daring deed, her amusement died. She began to see a pattern that alarmed her and sent her spirits plummeting. He had always sought excitement and adventure. From the day he started walking, trouble had been his destination.

She stole a glance at Patrick as he laughingly refuted one of Jeannie's claims. He was secretly proud of his feats. She could see it in his face, hear it in his voice. She realized that skippering racing yachts on the ocean wasn't just a passing fancy. Though he might stop for her sake, he would always gravitate toward adventure—and danger. It was bred in his bones. If not sailing, he would find something else.

Kate looked down at the remains of the meal in front of them, then at the people seated around the table. Laughter abounded. Jeannie's husband, Charlie, had joined them, sitting close to his wife and stroking a hand over her back. Evan sat at one end of the table tossing a ball for a large black Lab. He had added some of the more hair-raising details to the stories. Children raced back and forth from the grass to the table with either complaints or triumphs. It was the picture of a happy, loving family.

Evan was partly right; by themselves, Patrick's family had the power to change her mind. But Kate couldn't dismiss the stories she had heard. Patrick might change his travel schedule to be with her and the baby, but he could never change who he was. She didn't want a daredevil or a vagabond for a husband, no matter how terrific the family that produced him.

Kate rose to her feet and smiled at everyone. "This has been lovely, but I'm afraid I have to leave."

Patrick took her hand. "Not yet, Katie."

"We're all going for a swim," Evan said, a devilish glint in his eyes. "Don't you want to stay for that?"

Kate glared at him. "Too bad I didn't bring my suit."

"It was great meeting you," Jeannie said. "I'll call Patty and we'll plan dinner together some night."

Kate smiled but didn't answer. She began stacking the plates as everyone rose. Ian brought a trash can over and the table was cleared in moments. He dropped a kiss on her cheek.

"See you soon, Kate."

"Bye, Ian."

As she moved across the grass, Patrick fell into step beside her. "Thanks for coming, Katie."

"You have a very nice family."

He smiled. "Nice, loud and sometimes obnoxious," he said with a laugh. "I hope they didn't overwhelm you."

"No." Kate paused. "They're really different from mine, though."

"What's your family like?" Patrick's eyes were alight with curiosity. "You don't talk much about them."

She shrugged. "Small and quiet."

"No wonder you're ready to leave."

Kate remained silent. When they reached her car, she opened the door and was hit in the face with a blast of trapped heat.

"Give it a minute to cool." Patrick pulled her away from the vehicle into the shade of a nearby tree.

He ran his hands over her arms, sending a shiver across her skin. This close, the aroma that was Patrick Berzani tantalized her. She wanted to bury her nose in his neck and nibble a path upward to his ear, tasting and tempting him in equal measure. Patrick seemed to sense her desire and his eyes turned dark in answer.

"Can I come over tonight?"

Kate swallowed hard, tempted to say yes. It would be so easy. Just say yes and she would have Patrick, and if not him, at least his family. She had to admit the combination was very potent. If she could not create her own family, she might choose the Berzani clan. But what would that mean for her child? At the best, she would grow up longing for a father she seldom saw. At worst, Patrick would die in one of his daredevil feats and the baby would never know her father at all.

Slowly, she shook her head no.

"Why not?"

"Did you listen to the stories your family told about you?"

Patrick frowned. "Of course I did. I've heard them a hundred times. What are you—"

"In every one, you're the kid who always pushes the envelope. *You* are the kid in jeopardy. You encourage others to follow along, get them to do things they wouldn't dream of trying on their own."

"Maybe that's true. So?" He was still frowning.

Kate sighed and ran a hand over her hair, tucking a loose strand behind her ear. "You're an adventurer, Patrick, in the true sense of the word."

"I don't see what this has to do with me coming over tonight," he said impatiently.

"I know." Kate stared at him for a long, silent moment. "You're never going to change, Patrick. After today, I don't think you can. You're always going to push limits and try new things. Giving up sailing for me and the baby won't make you any different."

"Kate, those were stories about a young boy." Patrick put his hands on her shoulders, squeezing slightly. "Every kid gets into trouble, tests the boundaries. Well, maybe I did push them further than most," he added with a coaxing smile.

"And you still do," she said.

Patrick shook his head, his face serious. "Not like that. The ocean's no place to be cocky."

"Then why can't you quit? Stay home. Work in your family's marina?"

"I suppose because sailing is part of who I am," he said quietly.

"And you love it. I've seen the look on your face when you talk about racing. Your eyes light up like someone plugged you into an electrical socket."

"I *do* love racing, but I can cut back on it, so I'm here more than I'm gone."

Kate took a step away and hugged her arms around herself. She felt cold, despite the heat of the afternoon. "I don't think you should," she said.

Patrick was plainly astounded. "What?" he asked, shaking his head.

"It would be wrong for you to give up what you love. It's also wrong for me to ask you. It would just be a matter of time before you hated me for tying you down."

Patrick was silent, watching her, his face still. He made no attempt to touch her again, but shoved his hands into the pockets of his shorts. A car passed by and pulled into a slot farther along. The people got out and walked off with only a brief glance at Kate and Patrick.

"Why does this sound like goodbye?" he asked. His voice was quiet and deep, hard to hear over the shouts of the children in the park.

"Maybe because it is?" Kate's voice was a whisper, too. She didn't want to hurt him, but she knew her words sliced like a jagged knife. "I can't live with a man like that. I can't have him be the father of a child that I love. I'm sorry, but I can't."

Kate looked away, toward the pavilion. Fewer people were left now. Most had gone down to the beach to swim.

"How can you throw everything we have away so easily?"

"This is not easy, Patrick!" Tears welled up in her eyes and she blinked them back. "But we can't ignore the truth about who we are. Too much is at stake. I'm sorry," she said again. "I truly am."

Kate turned and walked quickly to her car. Patrick didn't try to stop her. As she pulled out of the parking lot, she took one last look in the rearview mirror. Patrick was standing where she had left him, hands in his pockets. He looked so lonely and sad.

A tear trickled down her cheek as she resolutely turned her attention to the road in front of her. She wiped the sadness away. She wouldn't cry. From now on, she would look to the future. She must. Her baby depended on it. But the tears still persisted, a soft rain of sorrow that wouldn't stop. Would she ever be over Patrick Berzani? Her heart whispered no, but Kate refused to listen.

Chapter Six

Patrick stood at the helm of the sailboat, feeling the rhythm of the waves through the wheel. He reached over and gave the winch another couple of turns, trimming the jib taut. *Blue Magic* picked up speed immediately, flying over the water. With one foot braced on the seat, he looked up at the mast, checking the rake. The backstay needed a bit more tension. A few pumps on the hydraulic adjuster took care of it and improved the shape of the sails, too.

Setting the autopilot, Patrick made a trip up the leeward deck, checking the tension of the shrouds. They all seemed to be loose enough without being too slack. He stopped at the mast and sighted up along its length. The rake was right, now. He looked at the foresail. The laminated fabric gleamed golden in the sunlight as it absorbed the power of the wind.

Back in the cockpit, Patrick took the wheel again. Wind and water were in concert, pushing the boat forward. Out here, he felt completely alive, his senses alert and his body in tune with the boat. Knowing what to do when the wind veered or backed was instinctual, as much a part of him as breathing. Kate was right; he had been born and bred to sail. How could he ever give it up, even for her?

All he had done for the past few days was think about

Kate, the baby and his future—*their* future. He still had no idea what to do. She was right about another thing. If he gave up racing for her sake, he would feel bitter about it, and maybe even put the blame on her. Part of his soul would die if he couldn't be out here on a day like this, pushing himself and a boat over the water.

Patrick went forward to make another check of the rig. Everything looked shipshape. He stood at the mast, surveying the horizon and thinking. Sure, he could cut back on his time at sea, but that wasn't enough for her. She was adamant; she wanted him to be around all the time or not at all. And what if he did what she wanted, would she start to nag him about taking unnecessary risks, too? *Be careful of the lawn mower, honey. Watch yourself on those steps.* Imagining these possibilities, Patrick could almost feel the chains wrap around his freedom. He shivered, despite the heat and went to the wheel again.

He remembered what Kate had said about him being an adventurer. He had denied it, but now he knew she was at least partly right. He did like to challenge himself, but that didn't make him some crazed adrenaline junkie, no matter what she thought. He wasn't doing it for the thrill. He just couldn't see doing things halfway, especially on something as beautiful as a boat, making her way over the water with all her sails set.

He tacked the boat over and kept going around, easing the sails into a broad-reach to retrace his course. Going downwind, the motion of the boat was gentler. No other boats were nearby, so he sat and let the gentle motion of the boat soothe him. Pulling his hat off, Patrick raked a hand back through his long hair. He needed a haircut soon, but not if he pulled it all out in frustration.

He had doubts about his abilities as a father, too. A whole truckload of doubts. Until he'd learned about Kate's pregnancy, the idea of becoming a father had crossed his mind as something hypothetical, a role he might consider taking on someday. Well, that day had arrived. Whatever his doubts and uncertainties, Patrick was sure of two things. Whether he was ready or not for the job, he would put everything he had into parenting. If Kate would let him. He just had to figure out a way to convince her that she should. He was also certain that no man could raise his child as well as he could.

As he approached the marina, Patrick furled the sails and turned on the engine. It started easily and ran smoothly now. Whatever had been wrong was fixed. He keyed the microphone on the VHF radio and called for a dockhand to handle lines as he motored around the breakwater. At the dock, he slid the boat smoothly into the slip, reversing the engine to stop it in place and tossed the mooring lines to a young man waiting there. In minutes the boat was secured.

"Thanks, Bill," Patrick said.

"My pleasure. I saw you coming in. She looks beautiful."

"She sails as good as she looks."

"You need anything else?" Bill asked.

"No, thanks. I'll just lock her up and put the covers on."

With a brief salute, Bill jogged up the dock, the radio at his waist squawking, directing him to some other task. Patrick smiled. The kid had more energy than two guys. He hoped his folks could convince him to stick around for longer than the summer.

Patrick had just finished buttoning up the mainsail cover when he was hailed by a tall, lanky man with graying hair.

"Patrick! How's my baby doing?"

"Hey, Jimmy." Patrick hopped off the boat and greeted the older man. "I think she's ready for her first lesson. How about if you clear your schedule tomorrow morning and we'll take her out?"

"That's what I want to hear." Jimmy rubbed his hands together and chortled. "Consider it cleared."

Patrick laughed. James Steele Johnson sounded like a kid on Christmas Eve. The childish glee seemed odd for a fifty-year-old man, but even the biggest boys loved getting toys.

"Be here at eight. The wind's supposed to hold through early afternoon, so we'll put her through her paces and get you familiar with all the systems."

Jimmy looked regretfully at the sleek blue craft. "Too bad we can't just take her out for a spin right now."

Patrick shrugged. "Why not? I've got the time."

"Don't tempt me. I've got a dinner date this evening. I'd be scalped if I stood her up for a sail."

"Your call." Patrick tightened one of the lines on the cleat and the two men walked up the dock together. "So who's this hot date that's coming between you and your boat? You still seeing Jill?"

"Nah. This is someone new. You might know her. Kate Stevens, the glassblower. She has that store FireWorks over on Oak Street."

Patrick clenched his jaw and stopped dead in his tracks. "So, you're candidate number two."

Jimmy surprised him by laughing. "That's what her aunt called me when I stopped by there yesterday. Bachelor number two, I think she said."

Patrick looked away, out toward the docks, debating what to say next.

"What's wrong?" Jimmy asked.

"Nothing." Patrick bit his tongue and held his ground. He felt like doing damage to any man who touched Kate. But this man was a client. And a friend. "Have a good time," he said flatly.

"You sure you don't want to tell me something?"

"It's nothing. I'll see you tomorrow." Patrick started to walk to his truck, then turned back. "Hey, Jimmy?"

"Yeah?" The older man was still looking at him.

"Do you know about Kate's… I mean do you know she's—" Patrick stumbled on the question.

"Do I know she's pregnant?"

"You know?"

"Yeah. So?"

"So you're still going out with her?"

"Why wouldn't I?" It was Jimmy's turn to look surprised. "I like her. She's pretty, sexy, intelligent."

"Do you know *why* she wants to go out with you?"

"Of course. And I'm honored she'd consider an older guy like me." Jimmy took a few steps closer. "Truth is, Patrick, I can't have kids of my own, so it's an opportunity to be a father. Never thought I'd have the chance." He shrugged. "I guess I was a little shocked at first when she told me the deal, but I like Kate's spunk. When I had a chance to think it over, I realized that I've got a lot to pass on to someone. Doesn't matter if it's my genes or not."

Patrick shifted uncomfortably.

"What's wrong? You got a problem with me going out with her?"

"Yeah, Jimmy," Patrick said with a sigh. "I have to admit I do."

"Why? Are you bachelor number three?"

"No. Near as I know, I'm not in the running." Patrick expelled a blast of air from his lungs. "My turn to tell the truth, Jimmy. The kid's mine."

Jimmy's eyebrows shot up. "Yours?"

"Yeah."

"Then why is she looking for a father? And a husband, for that matter?" Jimmy narrowed his eyes on Patrick. "Did you dump her?"

"No!" Patrick had a sudden urge to punch his truck again. "No," he repeated, reminding himself that none of this was Jimmy's fault. "Look, it's…it's between Kate and me."

Jimmy laughed. "Not anymore, man. Not if she's asking me to be the father. What's she got against you anyway?"

Patrick ran an impatient hand through his hair. "Kate doesn't think I'll be a good father. That I'm too much in love with sailing. I'm trying to convince her she's wrong, but she's not listening."

The older man looked at him for a long, silent time. "Then you need to try harder."

"I have been, trust me. Seems like I've run out of options."

Jimmy hesitated, then he spoke. "Portside Yacht Club, seven o'clock."

"What?"

"Better get cleaned up quick or you'll be late," the older man said tersely.

"You sure?"

"I think the real father deserves the first crack at this. If you want to make it work, I'm not going to stand in your way—regardless of what I want for myself."

A grin spread across Patrick's face. He put out his hand and gripped Jimmy's tightly. "I owe you for this, man."

"You got that right. I'll have to think of something for payback."

Patrick thought for a moment. "How about my America's Cup jacket."

"What? No way!"

"You heard me." Patrick's smile was wide. "This means a lot to me, Jimmy."

"But you can't replace something like that."

"I can't replace someone like Kate, either." Patrick

laughed. "Besides, I'll get a chance to earn another jacket someday. Next time, it might even say Captain on it."

"You must be serious about her."

"I am. I'll bring you your jacket tomorrow."

With a brief salute, Patrick turned and walked away. When he was halfway across the parking lot, Jimmy called out to him.

"Good luck. And don't screw up this time."

Patrick laughed and shook his head. Not this time. He had been given another chance. This time, he knew how to use it.

KATE SAT toying with the silverware on the linen-draped table. She looked at her watch again: seven-ten. She was hungry, and she hoped Jimmy wouldn't be too late. The baby bounced impatiently, bringing a smile to her lips. Apparently she wasn't the only one waiting for food. She smoothed the skirt of her dress over her thighs and subtly checked to see that the neckline hadn't slipped.

When she had pulled the dress out of the closet, it seemed perfect for the evening. Black, with a soft ruffle along the neckline, the Empire-style was loose and comfortable, but still dressy enough for the yacht club. Putting it on, Kate had eyed the décolletage dubiously. Was it lower than she remembered, or was there just more of her to fit inside? Pregnancy had made changes to more parts of her body than just her stomach. She had decided to wear it anyway, but kept checking to be sure she was covered.

A commotion at the entrance caught her eye. Kate did a double take when she saw Patrick threading his way through the tables toward her. The maître d', mouth pursed in disdain, followed close at his heels. Almost as astonishing was the extra-large, navy-blue jacket that Patrick wore over his green polo shirt and khaki trousers. She had never seen him in a sport coat, especially one so ill fitting. A red-and-gold-striped tie, knotted halfway down its length, hung loosely around his neck, too. The getup looked ridiculous, but rather than laugh, Kate found herself blushing. Even in those clothes, Patrick looked gorgeous. Heads turned and a low susurration of comments followed his passage through the dining room. When he reached her, he bent and kissed her cheek.

"Good evening. Sorry I'm a bit late." His hand collided with the maître d's as they both moved to pull out the chair opposite hers. "Thanks, man. I've got it."

The maître d' gave a twitch of his lips in a brief semblance of a smile and stepped back. When Patrick was seated, he handed him a menu and draped a cloth napkin across his lap.

"Your server will be with you shortly." He turned on his heel and left.

Kate watched the ritual with her mouth open. She was at a complete loss for words. Patrick laid down the menu and smiled at her, leaning his elbows on the table.

"What are you doing here?" she finally managed.

"Joining you for dinner, obviously." He paused and ran his eyes over her in a caressing stroke she could feel like a physical touch. His glance lingered on the low scoop of her neckline before rising to meet her eyes again. "You look gorgeous."

"But…but, you can't stay! I'm having dinner with someone else," Kate sputtered.

"Right. Jimmy told me to tell you that he's sorry but he couldn't make it. He mentioned something about taking out a sailboat."

"Why is this happening to me?" Kate put her hands over her face, as if blocking out the sight of Patrick.

The server chose that moment to arrive. She smiled at

them brightly, with only a slight pause as she noted Patrick's odd attire. "Welcome to the Portside Yacht Club. My name is Marnie and I'll be taking care of you tonight. Can I bring you something to drink? We have an extensive wine list, including several champagnes available by the glass."

"Kate, what would you like?" Patrick raised his brows. When Kate lowered her hands and simply stared at him, he smiled at the waitress. "Give the lady some sparkling water and I'll have a beer. Whatever you have on tap."

"We have thirteen beers on tap, sir," the waitress said with a smile. "Harp, Bass—"

"Just bring me a Yuengling. Bottle or draft, doesn't matter."

"Certainly." With a little bow, she backed away from the table.

Patrick turned back to Kate. "It's the clothes, isn't it?" He ran a thumb under the large lapel. "Just ignore them. I am. I had time for a haircut, anyway." He ran a hand over his freshly trimmed hair and looked around, meeting the eyes of several diners who stared back. He nodded briefly at one or two he obviously knew. Some acknowledged the greeting, others looked quickly away. Kate could see a grimace on his lips. "I remember now why I don't come here."

"Patrick." Kate took a deep breath and gathered her scattered wits. "I am not having dinner with you here."

"You want to go somewhere else?" He pushed his chair back. "Just say the word."

"I don't want to go anywhere with—"

The waitress returned with drinks on a tray. She carefully placed a glass on the table in front of Kate, then set a bottle of Perrier next to it, along with a small bowl filled with lime wedges. In front of Patrick, she set a stemmed glass of amber brew.

"We have a few specials that aren't on the menu tonight," Marnie began.

"Could you come back in a few minutes?" Kate cut her off with a tense smile.

"Sure, not a problem." The waitress darted a look between the two of them and left.

Kate turned to face Patrick, who had scooted closer to the table once more. He took a sip of his beer, avoiding her eyes. She didn't know what his game was, but she refused to play. "I am not having dinner with you. We said goodbye last Saturday. It's over between us."

Patrick looked back at her, his silver eyes unreadable. "Jimmy thinks I should give it another try."

"I don't care what *Jimmy* thinks."

"I think you'd better care, if you want him to become the father of my child."

Kate opened her mouth to speak, but Patrick beat her to it.

"Have you noticed that we've done nothing but argue since I got back to town?" He ran a hand over his face, as if tired to the bone, and lowered his voice. "I have an idea. Why don't we call a truce tonight? Set the clock back and pretend nothing's changed."

Kate sighed, infected by his weariness. "But everything *has* changed, Patrick."

"I know, but you've had time to figure out what you want and adapt to it. I've had a week and a half. I'm only human. I've screwed up. I admit it. You've got to cut me some slack."

Kate was silent a moment considering this, not wanting to feel sorry for him. "What exactly do you want from me?"

"Time." He pushed his beer aside and leaned forward. "We keep saying we need to talk, but we never do. Something interrupts or we end up fighting. I just want some time together so we can figure out if we can make it work. We've been apart for months, Katie. Don't you think we deserve a chance to get to know each another again?"

Kate avoided looking in his eyes, afraid that if she did, her heart might open to him just a little too far. "Time is something I don't have, Patrick. There's a baby on the way."

He shook his head and laughed softly. "You are so predictable sometimes." He reached across the table and took her hands. "You don't need to plan every second of your life, Kate. That baby won't be born for months. If I only ask for tonight, can't you afford to give me that much?"

He stood and drew her to her feet. Quickly, he shucked the jacket and tie, then draped them over his chair. Tossing a twenty-dollar bill on the table for the waitress, he took Kate's hand again and led her toward the door. "Do you have your car here?"

"No, Jimmy said he'd take me home. I caught a ride with Molly."

"Good."

Outside the club, Patrick gave his parking claim to the valet. He held her hand, but didn't speak as they waited for the truck to be brought to the curb. A low growl sounded from her stomach.

"Hold on, Junior," he said, patting her belly. "We'll feed you soon."

"Patrick, stop!" Kate blushed and ducked away from his hand.

The valet pulled up in the truck and Patrick handed Kate inside carefully. Seconds later they were on the road, headed out of town.

"Where are we going?"

"The Millside Inn. Hope you like great seafood."

"Of course. Is it far?"

"No, just over on Mill Creek. About fifteen minutes away."

"Good. I'm starving."

Patrick laughed. "That makes three of us."

As they rode in silence through the city and out into the suburbs, thoughts spun through Kate's head. What was she doing with Patrick Berzani? Couldn't she learn to say no to him? Tonight, she didn't want to. She wanted to believe whatever he said. Once they crossed the bridge over the Severn River, the houses thinned out and trees shaded the road. Soon, they were turning onto an even smaller road, then into a gravel parking lot. Patrick squeezed his truck into a narrow spot at the end of a long line of cars.

"You'll have to slide over and get out on my side."

Kate did and Patrick lifted her out of the truck and down to the ground. He held her with both hands at her waist, gazing into her face. Kate's hands were on his shoulders and she felt an overwhelming urge to slide them up and around his neck. She remembered how good his arms had felt wrapped around her at the picnic. Patrick stepped back before she could act on her impulse. Then he draped an arm around her shoulder and snuggled her up into his side. Slowly, she put her arm around his waist. She should push him away, but she didn't.

The small, waterside restaurant was thronged with diners. An outside deck wrapped three sides. Umbrella-shaded tables packed the space there. Waitresses wove intricate patterns through the tables, trays of crabs held high overhead. "Maryland Blue Crab, our special of the day, every day" read a motto on the sign just inside the door. A hostess dressed in tight shorts, with hair as straight and stiff as a board, led them to a small table off to the side. Seconds later a waitress buzzed by their table.

"What'll it be, hon," she asked in a nasal twang.

"A glass of ice water for the lady, a Yuengling for me, and a dozen crabs with the works."

"Youse want coleslaw or potato salad?"

"Both," Patrick said.

The waitress nodded and scribbled on her pad. "Johnny! Set 'em up over here."

Kate took in the view of Mill Creek, then of her companion seated across from her. "You've been here before."

"We used to sail up here when I was a kid." Patrick gestured to several sail and power boats bobbing at anchor. "It wasn't this crowded, but almost. I don't think the menu's changed at all since then."

Looking around at the crowds of people, Kate saw how her black cocktail dress clashed with all the shorts, T-shirts and bathing suits. Even Patrick's polo shirt and khaki trousers looked formal. Still, no one gave them a second glance. Unlike the yacht club, people were here to have a good time and eat good food. They didn't care who sat next to them or how they dressed.

A young man with a bleached-blond buzz cut came up to their table. "Crabs?" he asked.

Patrick nodded and leaned back to give him enough working room to spread a piece of heavy, brown butcher's paper over the table. He creased the corners and taped them in place. Next came two sets of wooden mallets, crab crackers and a roll of paper towels on an upright spindle. The young man left without another word. Moments later, the waitress plunked two glasses on the table. Beer foamed over the edge of one and dampened the brown paper.

They took a sip of their drinks and food started to arrive. First, a tray of crabs which the waitress spilled out onto the paper. Steam rose from the shells crusted with Old Bay Seasoning. She spun away, but was back in seconds with salads, corn bread, corn on the cob and soft, hot dinner rolls.

Kate tore off a length of paper towel and tucked it into the neck of her dress. "I didn't exactly wear proper attire for the occasion."

Patrick picked up a crab and turned it over, exposing the pale underbelly. He deftly pulled up a section of the carapace, pulled off the top shell and split the thing in two. "How does one dress for eating crabs?" He shot her a smile, one dark eyebrow raised in question.

"In clothes that can be hosed down." Kate cracked her own crab, sending juice splattering across the table and onto Patrick's shirt. "Oops."

He laughed and kept eating. "Watch out. Your turn might be next."

The meal was messy and delicious. Soon, they were up to their wrists in Old Bay and crab juice. It was a far cry from the refined meal Kate had expected at the yacht club. Perhaps better. And she decided, as she laughed and talked with Patrick, that she was having a much better time, too. It was like other meals they had once shared, months ago, before life had gotten complicated. For once—for one night—she was going to do as Patrick suggested and enjoy herself and his company. So far, she was having no trouble doing that, none at all.

Chapter Seven

A gentle breeze blew across the table, setting tendrils of Kate's hair dancing around her face. The busboy had cleared away the remains of dinner by simply folding the paper tablecloth in on itself and whisking the entire mess away. Now they sat sipping a second drink. The remnants of a dish of peach cobbler sat on the table between them. The crowd at the restaurant had thinned and it was quieter than before, but the pace would pick up again soon, judging by the band that was setting up inside.

Kate leaned her elbows on the table and looked out at the sparkling lights of the boats. Patrick's eyes traced the delicate planes of her face. Long lashes concealed the darkness of her eyes. Those eyes, deep brown and sparkling, had held him captivated all evening. Her rosy lips tempted him to lean over the table and kiss them.

He let his gaze travel down to the plump curves of her breasts where they rose above the neckline of her dress. A necklace of twisted green and blue glass nestled in the notch there. Matching earrings swung above, revealed by her upswept hair. His fingers itched to delve into the golden mass, pull the pins loose and send it tumbling down around her shoulders. His heart wanted to forget about their differences and bask in this moment forever.

Kate looked back at him and smiled. "This was fantastic. Better than the yacht club. Thank you for bringing me here."

"Thank you for not walking out on me at the club."

A slight flush rose in her cheeks and she looked away. "It crossed my mind."

Patrick smiled. "I know. You handled the surprise well." Beneath the tabletop, he clenched and unclenched his fists in indecision. "Why is it—" He stopped, uncertain that he wanted to continue.

"Why is what?"

He took a drink of beer and set the glass down carefully. Kate kept looking at him, a quizzical gleam in her eyes, but he avoided her gaze. One wrong question could lead to another argument, and that was the last thing he wanted right now. They were at peace tonight and he wanted to keep it that way.

"What, Patrick?" she asked again, touching his hand lightly.

Catching her fingers in his, he laced them together. Jimmy had given him this chance. He had to take some risk. "Why is it so important that I'm around all the time?" he asked, locking his eyes on hers.

"A child needs a father, Patrick," she said quietly.

"Agreed, but there's more to it, isn't there?"

She looked away, out over the water.

"Tell me, Katie," he urged. "I need to understand."

She sat still for a long time, drinking in the silence. When she looked back at him, her face seemed sad. "I suppose I don't want my child to miss her father the way I missed mine." She smiled, but it didn't reach her eyes.

"Why was he gone? His job?"

"It was more like his whole life." She shifted restlessly.

"What did he do?"

"He had a business. Still does. I guess you would call him a corporate raider."

"Like in the movies?"

Kate shook her head, chuckling a little. "A bit like that. Maybe not so exciting or sinister. Just a little sleazy. He buys companies that aren't doing so well, installs his own management team, fires some people, hires others and turns the company around and sells it."

"You don't sound too enamored with his methods."

"I'm not. A lot of people get hurt in the process."

"But isn't he ultimately helping people? I mean, if the company is doing badly and he makes improvements, that's better in the long run, right?"

"That's one way of looking at it, but it seldom works that way. Basically, my dad's in it for the money. He doesn't care about the people involved." Kate took a sip of her water. "I doubt he ever lost sleep over any of the people he fired or the careers he might have ruined."

"He doesn't sound like a very nice guy."

"He isn't. At best, he's a charming opportunist. Corporate *raider* is not a term of affection," she added drily.

"And his work came first. Family second."

"Or third or fourth. I'm not sure. He lived in his Lear. We saw him on the occasional holiday and the odd weekend when we flew out to wherever he was."

"That must have been fun, traveling all over the place."

"Mmm. I can describe the decor in some of the finest hotels in the country. No. The traveling was boring. My mother worshipped him. She made us wait around for him in between meetings. We couldn't leave the hotel because, *what if he was free and wanted to see his precious children,*" she finished, her eyes wide in a parody of a concerned mother.

"He didn't spoil you?"

Kate turned her water glass around and around. "Oh, we had everything. Everything except a father who was there to hold your hand, pick you up when you fell. The sort of things fathers are supposed to do. I tried to be daddy's little girl, but trying to get his attention drained me. My brother never gave up. I think his first words were 'Watch this, Daddy.'"

"Wait a minute, you have a brother?" Patrick was surprised. "Where does he live?"

"He doesn't live anywhere," Kate said quietly. "He died four years ago."

Patrick squeezed the hand he still held. "I'm sorry, Katie."

"So am I." Her mouth lifted in a slight smile, but her eyes shimmered with tears. She sighed and looked away.

"What happened?"

She shook her head and kept her face turned toward the water, as though she was avoiding his gaze.

"Katie?"

She darted a glance at him, then looked back at the boats again. Her fingers squeezed his, then she drew her hand away. "His death was senseless and stupid. I'd rather not talk about it. Please? Not tonight. We're supposed to be enjoying each other."

Patrick watched her closely while she kept staring out at the boats as if they fascinated her. Whatever had happened was a key to her fears but, for tonight, too painful to unlock. He filed his question away for later.

The band started up with a blare of guitars backed by the deep bass throb of drums. The lead singer swung into "Old Time Rock and Roll," drawing everyone's attention, even Kate's. Couples piled onto the dance floor. Lights flashed and bodies twirled to the beat. Patrick noticed her body sway to the rhythm. Her fingers tapped on the table. Some of the sadness lifted from her face.

He stood and held out his hand to her. "Come on. Let's dance."

Kate looked up at him, her eyes startled. "Really?" Her smile chased the rest of the pain from her eyes. "Yes, I'd love to."

Patrick led her inside, weaving his way through the mass of bodies to a tiny spot of clear space on the dance floor. The music and the energy of the other dancers infected them. Kate moved her hips to the bass and sang along to every word. When she laughed aloud, her dark eyes shining up at him, Patrick shared her delight.

One song segued into another and another. Kate spun and twirled, bopped and shook. Patrick did his best to match her, but was often content just watching her. She looked so happy. And irresistible. For the first time since he had come back home, he was seeing her without shadows.

Finally, the band swept into a slow number. Kate flowed into his arms like a gentle river. He closed his eyes and drew her close, then closer still. Her arms encircled his neck, fingers lightly stroking over the back of his head, playing with the hair at his nape. Patrick pressed a kiss to the side of her throat. He felt rather than heard the laugh of pleasure she made.

She felt so good. He wanted to go on holding her forever. Her scent filled his head, warmed by the heat of her dancing. Pressed this close to her, he could feel the bulge of their child. Easily, as if he had done it a hundred times before, his hands slipped down her back to her hips, pulling her—them—into the protection of his body. Kate rocked against him slowly, driving him completely crazy. The song ended and she slipped away, leaving him burning for another chance to hold her. They danced through another fast one before Kate took his hand. He let her lead him back outside to their table, into the evening air that cooled his cheeks.

She sat down with a breathless laugh, then picked up her glass of water for a long drink. Her delight was evident. Her eyes were shining and a flush filled her cheeks.

"I haven't done this in forever." She smiled at him and reached out a hand. "I'm having a great time."

"We ought to do this more often." The tone was light, but Patrick meant every word.

Kate laughed.

A few minutes later, he tugged her to her feet once more. "Let's do it again."

He danced her through more songs, drinking in her laughter and the sight of her sensuously shifting body. When the band started another slow song, Patrick took Kate into his arms. He pulled back enough to look into her eyes before slowly lowering his mouth to hers. The fire was instantaneous. But it wasn't enough. He needed more of her than he could get on a dance floor.

He trailed kisses to her ear. "Let's get out of here."

When he lifted his head to look at her, Kate's eyes were half-lidded, desire plain on her face. This time, he led her back to their table, snagging the waitress along the way. When she brought the credit-card slip, Patrick added a tip and scribbled his signature. Finally, they threaded their way through the crowd. In the parking lot, Patrick pulled Kate close as they walked.

Once again, they were silent on the drive to her house, only this time anticipation kept them from speaking. Patrick held one of her hands, brushing a thumb over her wrist. In her strong pulse he felt the beat of his own heart.

He parked behind her house and helped her out of the truck cab. When he lifted her down, she let her hands slide up over his shoulders and around his neck. She stretched up on tiptoe as his mouth descended to hers. Their lips met in a greedy, hungry kiss.

The scent, taste, feel of this woman in Patrick's arms nearly overwhelmed him. He couldn't seem to touch her enough. His hands stroked over her back, her filmy dress the slightest barrier to his touch. He caressed down to her bottom and back up, relearning every dip and curve that he had once known so well. Heart pounding, his body tightened. Every nerve seemed afire.

He slipped a hand between them and cupped one breast gently. When he stroked a thumb over her nipple, she moaned. He kissed his way across her jaw to her ear, savoring the feel of her silky skin under his lips. The perfume she wore teased his nose, making him want to explore all the places where the wonderful scent might hide. Nibbling gently, he followed the column of her throat down to the plump flesh he cradled, then blazed a trail of kisses just above the frilled edge of her dress.

Kate gasped and tightened her hands on his shoulders. She pressed against him, arching herself into him. "Please, Patrick." Her voice was soft and aching with need.

He said nothing, but caught her lips in another hard kiss.

"More," she whispered. Her eyes met his in the darkness, gleaming with urgency. "I need all of you. Now."

With her words, Patrick's restraint snapped. He pulled her close and their mouths fused together in a kiss that rekindled all the passion they had snuffed for months. He thrust his fingers into Kate's hair, holding her head still for his plundering. The pins anchoring her hair in place scattered to the ground and the silken, scented mass tumbled over her shoulders.

With a groan, he lifted his mouth from hers. "Let's go inside."

Kate nodded. When she stumbled a little on the steps, Patrick picked her up and carried her to the door. There, he slid her down his body, pressing her against the panel and bringing both hands up to cup her breasts. Fabric impeded his touch too much now, so he reached around and unzipped her dress enough to pull the shoulder straps down. She wasn't wearing a bra. Pale flesh glimmered in the porch light and Patrick couldn't help staring at her beauty. Reverently, he held her breasts in his palms. The nipples were larger than he remembered, a deeper pink than before.

Kate gasped at the first touch of his hands on her skin. "Oh, Patrick."

"Does it hurt?"

"No," she whispered, laying her head back on the door panels. "It feels like I'm on fire."

Patrick swallowed hard. He bent his head and kissed each rosy bud before looking into her face once more. Kate's eyes were half-closed and a smile played upon her lips. If he hadn't known she only drank water that night, he would have thought she was drunk.

"I want to make love to you, Katie. Can I?" He splayed a hand over the bulge of her belly, hidden by the gauzy skirt of her dress. "Can *you?*"

Slipping her arms around his neck again, Kate stood on tiptoe and brushed her mouth against his. "Yes, Patrick. Yes to all your questions."

UNLOCKING THE DOOR and stepping into the dark house, Kate felt Patrick follow her inside. He closed the door behind him and placed a kiss on the back of her neck. Her dress still gaped open in the back, so he trailed his mouth down her spine, unzipping and baring more of her skin as he went. Once the dress was completely unzipped, the fabric slipped to the floor, pooling at her feet to expose her stockings, lacy panties and high-heeled shoes.

Patrick groaned. "You're killing me."

Kate laughed, low and seductively.

His hands came around and he pulled her back against his chest. "Don't tell me you dressed like this for *Jimmy.*" He sounded jealous.

"I didn't intend for anyone to see this," Kate reassured him, leaning her head back onto his shoulder as he fondled her breasts. She had thought that, being pregnant, she would be indifferent to sex. And with her stomach growing larger every day, she should feel fat, but when Patrick ran his hands over the bulge, all she really felt was sexy and filled with desire for more.

His hands dipped lower, slipped inside her panties and his fingers touched her lightly, delicately. She couldn't believe how good it felt. In an instant, before she knew what was happening, she felt an orgasm rush through her in a burst of power. She laughed, then sobbed, all the time shaking from the intensity.

As the shudders of pleasure ebbed, she found herself lifted and carried down the hall to her bedroom. Patrick laid her on the comforter, then reached over and flicked on the bedside light.

"I want to see you," he said, his voice hoarse. "All of you."

He held her eyes captive as he pulled off his shirt. Underneath were broad shoulders her hands itched to touch. The dragon tattoo that snaked around his upper arm snarled at her. She followed his hands as he unbuckled his belt, then unbuttoned his trousers. Slowly each tooth of zipper released.

Kate swallowed in anticipation, her mouth dry as she waited for him to reveal the rest of her prize. Her breathing shortened and it was all she could do to not reach out and grab him, tearing him free of what few clothes remained. Patrick's eyes teased her as he slowed the unveiling even more.

"Now you're the one killing me," she said on a sigh.

He laughed and leaned down to kiss her, hard and quick, then pulled back before she could grab him. "Don't worry. I know just the thing to bring you back to life."

He slipped his thumbs into the waistband of his black boxer briefs and pushed them, and his pants, down. His erection sprang free, thick and ready. Kate put out a hand to stroke him, but he evaded her grasp. The sight of him naked and just out of her reach made the breath hitch in her throat. Desire swamped her.

"Please, Patrick," she whispered. "I need you. I want to feel you pressed against me."

"Soon, darling. Soon."

With his clothes disposed of, he knelt on the bed beside her and took off her shoes. Next came her stockings, each one slowly rolled down as he placed a trail of kisses from thigh to toe tip. Kate couldn't keep still. Every touch of his mouth tingled and sent arcs of heat through her bones. She writhed and tiny gasps rose to her lips.

He kept himself just out of her reach, so she could only accept his attentions and revel in them. His light touch was unbearable torture, but Kate wouldn't have changed a moment of it. The anticipation drove her wild.

Patrick slipped her panties down her legs. He took a long, slow survey of her body, each touch of his eyes as tangible as a kiss. He reached out and smoothed a hand over her belly. Kate gasped and arched her back into the callused warmth of his touch.

"Are you sure?" he asked.

Kate smiled. "I've never been so sure." A thread of doubt crept into her mind and she searched his face. "Does it bother you?"

"Bother me?" Patrick asked. He lowered himself to the bed beside her, stretching out to lie against her full length. He stroked her belly again, this time allowing his fingers to drift lower. "That you're pregnant?"

He kissed her tenderly as his nimble fingers set her on fire. She could barely remember her question.

"Yes," she gasped. She reached out and wove her fingers into his hair, bringing him closer.

Patrick rose above her and fitted himself into her moist, welcoming warmth. Kate gasped at the glorious feel of him inside her. He braced his arms on either side of her head. She could tell he was being careful not to put his full weight down on her as he thrust. As he moved, he kept his eyes locked with hers. With each plunge he took her higher and higher.

Kate lifted her knees to let him slide deeper until he groaned in pleasure. The friction was so intense, as if her every nerve ending was twice as sensitive as usual. She felt herself spinning wildly out of control. In seconds, she reached the pinnacle and tumbled over it into ecstasy. Dimly, she heard Patrick's shout as he joined her.

Panting and sated, he laid his forehead on her shoulder. He shifted to the side to keep from crushing her. Kate reached out and gently touched the line of his jaw. Patrick turned his head to bury his lips in her palm. Slowly, their breathing returned to normal. Cuddled in each other's arms, Kate felt a contentment she hadn't in a long time, not since Patrick had last held her like this.

"No, Katie." His voice rumbled in her ear, startling her.

"No, what?"

He rose to one elbow and propped his head on his hand. Stroking a hand over her stomach again, he smiled. "It doesn't bother me at all that you're pregnant. In fact, maybe I like it better."

Chapter Eight

Sunlight eased its way into the room, first a glimmer along one windowsill, then a growing streamer of light over the floor. Kate rolled onto her back and sighed. The beam of sun found its way to her pillow then over her closed eyes. With a groan, she flung an arm across her face. It was no use. Daylight would not be denied and her eyelashes fluttered open.

Memories of the night before washed over her. Smiling, she stretched long and slow, savoring the friction of sheet against bare skin. She rolled onto her side, reaching out to Patrick. Her hands felt nothing but cold cotton; the space next to her was empty. She rose up on one elbow. He was nowhere in sight. Even his clothes were gone from the floor. The sunlight, now flooding the room, lost some of its bright cheer.

The door to the bathroom opened quietly and Patrick stepped through. His eyes met hers and he smiled, bringing the joy back to the morning.

"So, you're finally awake."

His teasing words sent a shiver down her spine. Kate pulled the sheet up around her breasts and sat up to face him. He tossed the towel hanging around his neck back into the bathroom and walked to the bed. As he came closer to her, she was vaguely aware that she was staring. Shirtless, his unbuttoned trousers hung low on his lean hips, he was a fantasy come to life. Her fantasy.

He sat beside her, one foot curled under him, one on the floor. "How'd you sleep?"

"Did we sleep?" Her voice was husky and low.

Patrick laughed, running a hand over her cheek and into her hair, pulling her close for a brief kiss. One taste was not enough. Kate leaned closer and kissed him back, holding his lips captive with her own. Patrick pulled away with a groan.

"I have to go, Katie."

Kate let go of the sheet and put her arms around his neck. Her breasts pressed to his chest, relishing the contact between them. "No, you don't," she whispered against his mouth.

Their lips fused as passion rose. Kate gasped when his hands cupped her breasts. Her back arched and her nails bit into the taut skin of his shoulders as he caressed and kissed her. Patrick rose on one knee and laid her on the bed, coming down to cover her.

"I have to go." He repeated the words against her skin, trailing a line of kisses down her throat. "Jimmy's waiting for me."

"Let him wait."

Patrick lifted his head to look into her eyes. He bent and kissed her again. "Let him wait," he agreed.

No more words were spoken as they touched, stroked and seduced each other. The passion between them flared just as hot as it had the night before.

Finally, Patrick lay panting at Kate's side. He raised his head to look at the clock and fell back with a groan. "Jimmy's going to kill me."

Kate looked over at him and smiled. Contentment filled her heart. "Well, I'd have killed you if you left. Which was better?"

With a laugh, Patrick rose and disappeared into the bathroom, grabbing his pants as he went. When he came out he was dressed and tucking his shirt into his waistband. He shoved his bare feet into brown leather boat shoes as he buckled his belt. Raking a hand through his hair, he came to the bed and leaned over her again.

"I'll come back as soon as I get done."

"Why are you meeting Jimmy?"

"We're test-sailing his boat." Patrick dropped a kiss on her lips. "It was his boat we went out on the other day."

Kate frowned. She remembered that day all too clearly. "Be careful."

He ran a finger lightly down her cheek. "It's not dangerous." His gaze was tender and his lips held a slight smile.

She wasn't convinced. "For my sake, be careful," she said again.

Patrick kissed her, this time longer, lingering and gentle. "I'll be back this afternoon." With that, he rose and strode to the door and out.

Kate sat up abruptly, clutching the sheet to her chest. "Patrick! I won't be here this afternoon."

He returned to the doorway. "Where are you going?"

"I have a doctor's appointment at two-thirty."

Patrick looked at her for a long, silent moment. His gray eyes were dark, his expression still. When he spoke, his voice was soft and low. "Can I come with you?"

Tears sprang to Kate's eyes. The door to her heart opened a little more to him and, this time, she didn't try to slam it shut. She nodded.

"I'll have to meet you there."

Kate swallowed past the lump in her throat. "Chesapeake Medical Center, on the fourth floor. Dr. Cassel's office."

"Two-thirty. I'll be there." With a nod, Patrick disappeared.

Seconds later, Kate heard the door slam and his truck start up right after that. She lay back on the bed and stared at the ceiling. The tears in her eyes slipped down her temples. Was she crazy? Her head said yes, but her heart said no. Her heart had been saying yes to Patrick Berzani for a long time. This time, she was going to listen.

"ARE YOU ALL RIGHT?"

"I'm fine." Kate caught the skeptical look in Molly's eyes. "Really. I'm fine," she repeated, more to reassure herself than her aunt.

She shifted in her chair. The padded vinyl seat was hot and sweaty against her thighs. She stifled a sigh and tried not to look at her watch again. Two-thirty had come and gone with no sign of Patrick. He hadn't even called. Kate told herself it was a good thing the doctor was running late, since Patrick was, too. But why hadn't he called?

"Kate Stevens?" Stephanie, Dr. Cassel's nurse, stood at the door to the waiting area. Dressed in pink flowered scrubs, she was a beacon of cheer in the drab room. She smiled and motioned to Kate. "Come on back."

Kate and Molly both rose to follow the slender woman down a long, wide hallway. A few open doors gave glimpses into examination rooms. The sharp, not unpleasant smell of disinfectant and alcohol teased Kate's nose.

"I'm sorry about the long wait," Stephanie apologized cheerfully as she led them to the end of the hall. Turning left, she stopped in front of a set of louvered doors across from a darkened room filled with equipment.

"We got backed up in the ultrasound room this morning and we're just starting to catch up. We've discovered two sets of twins today!"

Twins? Kate exchanged a look with Molly. "I hope you don't find that she's carrying the third set," Molly said.

"That would be a miracle for sure," the nurse said with a laugh. "You can change in here." She opened the louvered doors. Inside, against the far wall, was a bench with a fold of blue cotton on it. On one side, mounted high on the wall, were three hooks. A small shelf with a mirror over it faced them on the opposite wall.

"Put the gown on with the ties in front, and wrap the other cloth around your waist." She reached out and patted Kate's stomach affectionately. "And you still have one to wrap it around."

"Not for long," Molly said. "Her figure is disappearing faster than the ozone layer."

"I can still see my feet," Kate said with a frown. She felt irritated at Molly and the nurse joking about her body.

Stephanie smiled and stepped back. "When you're ready, come across to this room and we'll get started. You can have a seat in there now," she told Molly.

Kate stepped into the changing room, then turned back. "Stephanie?"

"Yes?"

Kate paused, biting her lip, and darted a glance at Molly. Heat rose in her cheeks. "If a man comes in looking for me, would you let me know? His name is Patrick. He's tall with dark hair."

"Is that Dad?" Stephanie asked. "I'll be sure to bring him back."

The nurse turned and hurried away, dropping the file she carried in the bin attached to the door of the ultrasound room. Kate went into the changing room, avoiding Molly's eyes. Inside, with the doors closed, she checked her cell phone one more time. Nothing.

Slowly, Kate sat on the bench and tried not to cry. Patrick wasn't coming, she told herself. And he wasn't going to call, either. He must be too involved in sailing and had either forgotten about her or else drowned in some accident. She almost hoped it was the latter. Feeling sorry for herself, she snatched a tissue from the box on the shelf and wiped her eyes, then balled it up and threw it in the trash. Rising, she changed into the loose gown and tied the long cloth belt across her protruding belly. The thin cotton made her feel exposed and vulnerable.

She looked at herself once in the mirror and scowled. Who was she trying to fool? What she wore had nothing to do with how she felt. Nor did Molly's or Stephanie's quips. Patrick made her feel this way: annoyed, irritated with herself, embarrassed, alone. She closed her eyes on a sigh. Last night in his arms and this morning's happiness seemed light-years away.

With a jerk, she opened the door and walked across to the other room. Molly sat on a chair chatting with another woman. When Kate came in, they both turned to her.

"You must be Kate," the chubby, older woman said. "I'm Delia. I'll be doing your ultrasound today." She rose and shook hands with Kate, her grip soft and warm. "Climb on up here and let's get started."

Kate got onto the padded table and lay back on the inclined rest. "I don't want to know what sex it is, okay? So if you see anything you recognize, don't tell me."

"Got it," Delia said with a smile.

The older woman's hands were gentle as she worked on Kate. Tears trickled down Kate's cheeks as she saw the shape of her baby on the monitor, tears of happiness; she had a wonderful, growing child inside her. She shed tears of sorrow; that child's father was not here as he had promised.

After Delia was finished, Kate changed into her clothes and joined Molly in the waiting room. Stephanie stood behind the desk.

"Delia got some lovely pictures," she said. "We'll see you next week for your regular appointment."

"Thanks, Stephanie." Kate nodded and turned to go.

"Sorry that Dad couldn't make it. I'm sure he'll be really bummed."

Kate nodded, unable to speak. She turned away, moving blindly, more tears flooding her eyes. Molly led Kate out of the office. She wrapped one arm around Kate tightly as they walked.

"I'm sorry, Katie," she whispered as they headed outside and into the parking lot. "I'm so sorry he wasn't here."

"He said he'd come." Kate couldn't help the gulping cry that sounded from her throat. "I t-told him where I would be and he *asked* me if he could come."

Standing beside her red SUV, Molly wrapped her in a close embrace, patting her soothingly on the back. "I know, sweetie. I know."

"He sounded like he wanted to be here. Like he cared." Kate pulled back to look into her aunt's eyes. What she saw there—pity, sadness and anger—didn't calm her own tangled emotions. "Why do I do this?" Kate whispered. "Why do I let him keep hurting me?"

"Because he's the father of your baby and, despite everything he's done—" Molly paused and stroked a strand of hair behind Kate's ear "—despite who he is, you love him."

"How can I love him? Why? We barely had two months together. That's nothing."

"Sometimes you know the first minute you meet someone that he's the one," Molly said. "You told me you felt that way about Patrick."

"I thought I did. I thought he felt the same, too." She shook her head as a fresh spate of tears fell. "But he didn't. He doesn't."

"He feels something, or he wouldn't keep showing up."

"It's not enough," Kate whispered, mostly to herself. "Whatever he feels, it's not enough. Not for me. Not for my baby." She swiped the tears away with her fingers, smearing them across her cheeks.

. Molly dug in her purse and handed her a crumpled tissue. "It's clean."

Kate took it, wiped her eyes, then blew her nose. "Let's go home."

The two women got in the car. Molly drove and kept up a stream of conversation at first, but Kate couldn't follow the words. Finally, Molly fell silent. As they turned into the driveway, Kate's phone rang. She stiffened. Her purse was in her lap, but she made no effort to open it and dig for the phone inside. She put one hand over the brown leather and felt the vibration as the phone begged her again and again to answer it.

"That must be Patrick. Are you going to talk to him?" Molly asked after the fourth ring.

Kate clutched the purse tightly and shook her head.

Molly looked at her for a long moment. "Do you want me to?"

Kate shook her head again. "No. He can leave a message." Her throat felt clogged with the tears she held in check.

The phone rang a sixth time. Molly opened her mouth then closed it. She nodded, pulled the keys from the ignition and got out of the car. Kate sat still, waiting, but the phone had stopped ringing. Slowly, she climbed out of the SUV. Sliding the straps of her bag over her shoulder, she shut the door.

From the depths of her purse, Kate heard a faint, two-toned beep indicating a message had been left. She opened the bag and grabbed the cell phone clipped to an inside pocket. When she flipped the phone open, "One Message" appeared on the screen. "Listen" or "Ignore," it prompted. Kate's thumb hovered over the buttons for a long moment. She finally pressed "Ignore" and closed the phone.

PATRICK GOT OUT of his truck in a rush, slamming the door without bothering to lock it. He took the stairs up to Kate's door two at a time. There, he knocked—hard. Leaning one hand against the jamb, he dropped his head, listening for some sound inside. He ran a hand through his hair, raking the damp strands back from his face, forcing himself to be patient.

The day was scorching hot. The high humidity made it seem even hotter. Pulling his T-shirt away from his chest, Patrick grimaced at the streaks of sweat striping the pale blue cotton and creating circles under his arms. There had been no time to change before rushing over here. He knocked a second time. It was all he could do to keep himself from beating down the door. He listened again, even pressing his ear to the wood, and heard nothing.

With a muttered curse, Patrick leaped back down the steps and headed for the studio. He reached the door and tried the handle. It was unlocked. Pushing the metal panel open, he stepped inside and closed it behind him, expecting to see Kate at work. But the furnace stood cold and silent. The light that bounced off the glass globes was the only thing moving in the room.

Then he heard the low hum of machinery, faint at first. He followed the noise to the room behind the ovens. There, Molly was hunched over a spinning potter's wheel. Dressed in faded green coveralls liberally smeared with clay, she was too intent on her creation to hear Patrick enter. Her elbows were braced on her knees while her hands smoothed and molded a whirling brown lump on the wheel. Occasionally, she would dip one hand into a pot of water next to the wheel, adding more liquid to the mess.

As Patrick watched, she plunged her thumbs into the center of the clay and drew them outward. A pot was created right before his eyes. She shaped the opening until it was the size of a silver dollar. Patrick moved closer for a better view. Molly looked up, startled. Her fingers slipped and the pot collapsed in on itself.

"Oh, Patrick, it's you." She flicked a switch with her foot. The wheel slowed and came to a stop. "You startled me."

"I have a bad habit of doing that. Last time I came in unannounced, Kate broke some glass."

Molly rose and wiped her hands on a brown-caked towel. "If you're looking for her, she's not here."

"When will she be back?"

"I have no idea. I'm not sure I'd tell you if I did."

Patrick could feel his temper fray. His day had not gone well and Molly's obstruction made it worse. "I need to talk to her."

Molly threw the towel aside and leaned against a table at the side of the studio. She folded her arms and looked him over. "What happened? Why weren't you at the doctor's office?"

"I got delayed."

"Then why didn't you call?" She pursed her lips, cocking her head to one side. "Maybe you just forgot about her again."

"I didn't forget!" Her sarcasm snapped something inside him. "My cell phone is at the bottom of the god-damned Chesapeake. Jimmy didn't bring his along and I couldn't get the radio to work, so I couldn't call."

"Hmm. Sounds plausible." She eyed him up and down. "I think I almost believe you."

"Just tell me where Kate is. Please."

Molly looked at him, her face expressionless. "She went out for a drive with Steve Craig."

The words hit Patrick like a punch in the stomach, sucking all the air from his lungs. He closed his eyes for a moment. "Why?"

"Why? Let me give you the short answer—because he showed up. You didn't. Steve came by right after we got home and asked her, so she went."

Patrick tried to stare at Kate's aunt, but his head was spinning almost as fast as her pottery wheel. He sagged against the wall and leaned back onto the brick, then took a few deep breaths. Molly didn't say another word, but he saw pity in her eyes. It felt like a handful of salt in his wounds.

"She was very upset when you didn't come to the doctor's office, Patrick." Molly sighed. "Maybe it wasn't your fault, but you really blew it."

"The engine broke down." He lifted his head and pleaded his case with the older woman. "Again. I had to sail the boat in. There wasn't any wind. I called when I got to shore, but she didn't answer."

"No. It was too late. She refused to."

They stared at each other for a long silent minute, then Patrick asked, "So what do I do now?"

"Give her time."

"And let someone else take my place? I don't think so."

"Patrick, you haven't *got* a place right now. Kate doesn't want anything to do with you."

"But I can't just let her go!" He straightened and paced the shop. "She has to let me explain. I would never have—"

"Whatever you say, she won't listen," Molly interrupted. "Do you know what you missed today? The first sonogram. The first time Kate saw her baby. I was honored to be there. It was a wonderful moment. She cried during the procedure. She cried afterward, too. But not because she was so happy. She cried because you weren't there to share that moment with her." Molly stopped and looked at Patrick, compassion warring with anger in her eyes. "Today, you confirmed every fear she has about you. By not showing up, you acted exactly like her father. He was never there for *anything* in that girl's life."

"But I tried. You don't know how hard I tried."

"I believe you," Molly said softly. "And maybe Kate will, too. In time."

"But I don't have time."

"Yes, you do." Molly came to him and laid a hand on his arm. "Please, Patrick. Leave Kate alone for a while. She's very fragile right now. She likes to think of herself as strong and tough, but her heart is like her glass. It shatters easily."

"I didn't mean to hurt her."

Molly shrugged. "Maybe not. But you did. Take my advice, let her heal. Then try again."

"You're asking too much from me."

"Believe it or not, Patrick, I'm rooting for you. At least most of the time."

Patrick squeezed Molly's hand in thanks, then turned and walked out of the studio without another word. He got in his truck and sat for a long while, deciding whether to wait for Kate or take Molly's advice. However right Molly might be about Kate's fragile heart, it was not the only one breaking. Eventually, Patrick stuck the key in the ignition and started the engine. He put the truck in gear and slowly drove home.

Chapter Nine

"How about if we stop for something cold to drink?"

"Sure, that would be great. It's really hot today." Kate winced as she unintentionally repeated her words of five minutes ago, but Steve seized on them like a lifeline tossed to a drowning man.

"I'll say. I've been working on a house out in Jessup. The air-conditioning isn't in yet and we've been roasting." He darted a glance at Kate. "Yep, pretty hot this year."

She was relieved to see the coffee shop ahead. Steve pulled the car up to the curb. They got out, walked across the sidewalk and up the steps in silence. She felt his hand hovering at her back for a moment as if he wanted to touch her, but then it dropped away. Instead he held the door for her. Inside, the cool air raised a rash of goose bumps on Kate's arms with tingling relief. She felt the heat more, the further her pregnancy advanced.

Only one table was occupied by a young man hunched over a laptop. Telltale cords led from the computer into his bushy hair. His head nodded rhythmically as his fingers tapped the keys. He sipped from a large mug that had a bright red glaze swirled with wide yellow curlicues—one of Molly's designs.

Behind the counter, a tall, lanky woman in black capri

pants, bright blue hair and red clogs rooted through a large refrigerator. She muttered to herself as she shifted plastic containers from one shelf to another.

"Good afternoon, Suzanne," Kate said.

The woman spun to face them, a wide grin splitting her face. "Kate, dear! How have you been?"

"Good. Love your ensemble. The apron almost matches your shoes."

The apron that encircled Suzanne's trim waist was pastel pink with a strawberry appliquéd on the front and stiffly starched ruffles. Suzanne held it with her fingertips for an exaggerated curtsy. "Direct from Milly Addison's garage sale. Her grandma made a bunch of them. I thought they added a touch of class to the joint," she said in a supercilious tone, then spoiled her act by giggling.

Her laughter was infectious, as always. Kate shook her head and Steve chuckled. "Milly's grandma is probably proud as peacock."

"She might be if she hadn't died about five years ago," Suzanne said. "So, what can I get you today?"

"Something cool. I'll have a glass of herbal iced tea," Kate said. "What's today's brew?"

"Chamomile and rose hips. You'll love it."

"And a large iced coffee for me." Steve handed her a ten.

Suzanne returned his change, then grabbed two glasses. "Have a seat. I'll bring them out to you."

Steve followed as Kate led the way to the table farthest away from the head-bopping man. The café was filled with an eclectic mix of furniture. Like Suzanne's apron, most were castoffs from garage sales. A bright chrome-and-pastel-pink dining set—complete with gold sparkles in the laminate—sat next to a scarred wooden table with mismatched chairs. Kate chose a table by the windows, this one sea-green with a lace pattern around the edges, and pulled out her chair.

Steve hastily grabbed the back of it from her. "Allow me."

Kate smiled her thanks and sat down, scooting forward as he pushed. Steve sat opposite her and folded his large hands on the table between them. Dusted with light blond hair, they sported several nicks and cuts from work. He laced his fingers together tightly as if he were nervous.

Suzanne brought their drinks over and set them on the table. "I added a little simple syrup. It brings out the flavor of the rose hips," she said, patting Kate's shoulder. "Anything else?"

"No, thank you. This is perfect."

Suzanne left the table.

Kate took a sip of her iced tea. "That feels so good. I think the heat's starting to get to me a little bit."

Steve's brow furrowed and his bright blue eyes took on a worried gleam. "That must be a problem in your studio."

"I think it's more the humidity. That's not a problem around the furnace."

Steve stirred his coffee, rattling the ice in the mug, and kept his eyes on his drink.

Finally, Kate could stand the silence no longer. She cleared her throat. "You surprised me today, Steve, when you stopped by. I guess I wasn't sure I'd see you again."

His eyes flew up to meet hers. "I—" He looked out the window as a red tide of color washed up his neck and into his cheeks. At last, he brought his gaze back to her. "Kate, I want to marry you."

She blinked at him in astonishment. "What?"

"I was an idiot that day, Kate." His hands reached out to clasp hers across the table. "I was just so surprised. I never expected something like that and I…" He squeezed her fingers in a hard grip as he swallowed. "I never dreamed you'd want me. I hoped, but…" He smiled slightly and shrugged as he let the words trail off.

This time, Kate was the one to look away. As she gazed through the window and across the street, she tried to make sense of the whirling emotions inside her. Was this what she wanted? One of the men she had picked to be her child's father was volunteering. She ought to say yes. She ought to be thrilled.

So why wasn't she?

She slipped her hands from his and put them in her lap. "I'm still pregnant with another man's child," she said quietly, keeping her eyes on his.

Steve curled one hand around the other. He rubbed his knuckles as he spoke. "I know that. And I'm willing to raise your baby just like it was my own."

She searched his eyes and saw only earnest determination. "Why?" She studied him intently. "Why the change?"

"Bottom line, Kate, I love you." His cheeks were red again, but his voice was steady. "I have since I first met you."

Kate hesitated before she spoke. She didn't want to hurt him, but she had to be honest. "I like you very much, Steve, but I don't love you. You understand that, don't you?"

"I know." He looked down, then back at her. "But who knows, maybe someday you'll feel the same way about me that I feel about you. That's enough for me."

His soft words brought a sting of tears. He was so kind, more kind than she deserved. Kate felt a wry sense of satisfaction. She may have failed with Patrick, but she had picked a good man this time.

The thought brought another possibility she had to warn him about. "Patrick may still try to be involved."

Steve shrugged again. He reached out for his glass,

but didn't lift it to his lips. "He's the father. He's got a right, I guess." His jaw jutted stubbornly. "But you would be my wife."

Kate opened her mouth to speak, then closed it. A lump in her throat kept her silent. She sipped at her tea, trying to wash it away. Yes, she would be Steve's wife. Why didn't that idea give her any comfort? *Patrick should be the one.* She closed her eyelids tightly, banishing the foolish wish from her heart. Just today, he had proved once again that, whatever he said, she and the baby took a distant second in his life. Still, she somehow couldn't simply say yes to the kind, generous man who sat across from her.

"I have to think about this."

"You do?" A line appeared between Steve's brows. "Why?"

"I just need some time."

"I thought you wanted me to marry you, to be your husband and a father." His eyes narrowed as he gazed at her. "Did I miss something? Has something changed?"

"I haven't asked you to do *anything,* Steve." Kate's voice was tart. "Either now or the last time I saw you. Remember that day? You were off the porch and gone before I could say a word."

Steve had the grace to look abashed. He sat back and raised his hands, palms out. "I know, I know. But I kind of got caught between you and Patrick that day. He tried to shock me, and he succeeded."

"I have to be certain you really want to be a father to another man's child." Kate held her hands out and he took them in a tight grip. "I don't want to make a mistake about this. I don't want you to, either."

"I'm not making a mistake."

"I want to be that certain." Kate squeezed his hands.

"That might take time, but I'm not going to rush this. Let's spend some time together and we'll see."

A broad smile spread across Steve's round face. "We'll make it work, Kate." His eyes were sparkling with excitement. "You'll see. I'll be a great father for your baby."

"I'm sure you will," Kate said, while she ignored the pang of sadness in her heart. It had been wrong about Patrick so far. From now on, she was going to listen to her head.

HOURS LATER, Kate was tired and irritable, locked in a tussle with her emotions. When Steve had brought her home, she had politely declined his dinner invitation. She promised to go out with him soon, kissed his cheek and shut the door behind him. It had been a long, stressful day and she wanted to lie down and decompress. Trying to nap proved fruitless, her thoughts too busy for rest. Now, unable to lose herself in a book or in mindless television, she sat eating ice cream, trying not to cry for the umpteenth time that day.

She had nearly polished off a bowl of chocolate-marshmallow swirl when a knock on her door startled her. She set the bowl down on the glass coffee table and rose to answer it. Kate peeked through the door to see her porch light illuminating Ian Berzani's face. She unlocked the door and pulled it open.

"Ian! What are you doing here?"

"Hey, Kate." He smiled and put his hands in his jeans pockets, shifting from one foot to the other. "Can I come in?"

"Sure. Why not?" Kate stepped aside. "Come in."

Ian followed Kate into the living room and looked around casually at the white walls dotted with colorful paintings. Then he examined the intricate blown-glass bowl in swirls of red and amber that stood on a pedestal between the two windows. "Wow, this is amazing. Yours?" he asked, keeping his eyes on the bowl.

"Yes, I just finished it a few days ago." She paused. "Your brother inspired it."

Ian stared at it for another, silent minute. "It's gorgeous, but you must have been really pissed at him."

Kate laughed, remembering the day she had made the bowl. "A pretty accurate assessment, I'd say."

With one last look at the piece, Ian turned to face her. "So he's good for something then."

Kate chose not to comment. "Have a seat." She gestured to one of the blue-denim sofas that faced one another across a tan-and-cream Oriental rug. "Can I get you something to drink? I've got iced tea or lemonade. There might even be a beer in the refrigerator." His eyes lighted on the bowl of melting ice cream and she smiled. "Or you can join me in some chocolate swirl."

"No, thanks, I don't need anything."

Kate took a seat facing Ian and pulled a throw pillow into her lap like a shield.

"I suppose you can guess why I'm here." He leaned back into the cushions, one foot propped on the opposing knee. He looked relaxed, certainly more so than Kate. She set the pillow aside and tried to mimic his insouciance.

"You're here because of Patrick. I knew that when I saw you on the porch." She bit her lip, but couldn't keep from asking, "How is he?"

Ian's voice was quiet, his eyes direct. "He's drunk."

Kate blinked, not sure she had heard him right. "Patrick? Drunk?"

"Evan found him on his boat curled up with an empty bottle of whiskey." Ian's lips lifted in a wry smile. "You obviously know that's not like him. He may be a sailor, but he's never been a drunken one."

"Why come to me about it?"

"Because even though Patty was pretty incoherent, Evan got enough out of him to lead me here." Ian's foot dropped and he leaned forward, placing his hands on his knees. "What happened today, Kate?"

She rubbed her forehead, suddenly feeling weary and annoyed. "Look, if Patrick is drunk, it's his own fault." She took a deep breath and let it out slowly, drawing the pillow onto her lap again and hugging it to her stomach. "I don't know what happened. Why don't you ask him after he sobers up?"

Ian's expression sharpened. "Did you have another fight?"

"No." Kate felt a blush climb her cheeks as the memory of their morning lovemaking swept over her. There was no pleasure left in it for her, only sadness and pain.

"How did Patty screw up this time?" Ian asked in a low voice.

The tears she had been fighting all day sprang up in her eyes again. One slipped down her cheek before she could wipe it away. Ian rose, came across to her and sat down. He put one hand over hers where she was tugging at the gold fringe on the pillow.

"Tell me, Kate."

"I had a doctor's appointment today." She lifted her eyes to his. "It was the first sonogram of the baby. Patrick said he'd meet me there, but he never showed up."

"He had to go out on a boat."

Kate nodded. "He told me. But he said he'd be done in time." She paused and swallowed back a sob. "He never even *called* to say he couldn't make it, Ian."

The words brought the memory of waiting for Patrick

into her mind, fresh and clear. More tears rose and she smeared them away as they fell. Ian handed her a faded blue handkerchief. He sat back on the sofa with a sigh, squeezing her hands once before he released them.

"That explains some of what Evan heard."

"About what?"

"Patty was going on about losing his cell phone." He looked at Kate. "Apparently, Jimmy's boat broke down again while they were out. If Patty lost his phone, he couldn't call you to let you know."

She could read the entreaty in his dark gaze and slid her eyes away from it. "It doesn't matter."

"Yeah, it matters, Kate. Patty didn't mean to miss the appointment."

Kate kept her eyes on the cushion she held. "If it wasn't today, it would have been some other time." Ian drew in a sharp breath, but Kate spoke before he could protest. "He's never going to settle down."

"Did he tell you that?"

"After the picnic on Saturday, I don't need to be *told,* Ian. You said yourself that he's always been a daredevil. A wife and child are the last things Patrick wants."

"Then why is he drunk on his boat right now?" Ian asked quietly. "He's as upset about this as you are."

Swallowing back more tears, she looked at Ian and shook her head. "I'm sorry. I just can't do this anymore. Every time I get my hopes up and think things will change, Patrick lets me down. I need him to put me and the baby first and he can't."

"He's trying, Kate."

She shook her head again. "I don't want him to try anymore. I just want him to leave me alone."

Ian's jaw flexed and she could see a nerve jump in his cheek. She expected him to lose his temper, but when he spoke, he was calm. "Imperfect as it is, Patty is doing the best he can. Please, just consider giving him another chance. I think you'll regret it for the rest of your life if you don't."

"I can't," she whispered.

Ian stood up and walked over to the glass bowl again. "He inspires you, Kate. Isn't that worth something?"

"He *inspires* rage, Ian. That isn't what I'm looking for in a father for my baby."

"But if he makes you that angry, what other emotions can he inspire in you?" he asked, looking over at her. His face was serious and solemn. "An emotion that powerful doesn't stand alone. There's always more underneath."

"I'm sorry, Ian. I know you want to help your brother, but there's nothing you can do, or say."

Ian walked back to face her, his hands in his pockets. He looked down at the floor, frustration written in every line of his body. "Think about it. Please. For your own sake. For the kid."

He turned and left the room. She heard the door open and close again with a soft click, then his boots on the stairs outside. Kate sat where she was, hugging the pillow to her chest.

She had no tears now, only a well-deep sadness. She tried to blank out Ian's words, but they rang in her head. She held the cushion tighter. She concentrated on her meeting with Steve that afternoon. He was her future, not Patrick. Closing her eyes, Kate took a deep breath. She and her baby would be happy, she vowed. With Steve they would be a family. There was nothing else she wanted. Nothing else, she told herself.

Chapter Ten

Kate added heat to the glass with the torch, blew into the soffieta and expanded the bowl of the goblet just a little more. Holding the piece up by the punty, she judged that it was balanced now. The plumper globe was more proportionate to the height of the stem. She was pleased with the color, as well. The thin, dark red belt of glass around the middle of the vessel stood out beautifully on the lustrous, silver-tinged Pyrex. She transferred it to a fork, tapped it off the punty and put it in the annealing oven next to three other goblets just like it.

Closing the door on the oven, Kate striped off her heat-proof gloves and wiped the back of her hand across her forehead. She sat on a stool and rested for a minute, pushing her goggles up onto her head. She hated how short of breath she was these days, but the doctor said that was nothing to be alarmed about. She was six-and-a-half months' pregnant. It was all part of the process. *Like having to go to the bathroom every five minutes,* she thought with a twist of her lips.

The door opened and Molly walked into the studio in a red dress dotted with yellow ducks. Her hair was its usual wild mess, pulled up today with yellow banana clips. "Hey, how are you?" Her smile was bright and cheerful.

"Fat. Pregnant." Kate leaned an elbow on the workbench and rubbed her lower back. "How are you?"

Molly laughed and came over to hug her. "Bad day, huh?"

Kate shrugged. "I'm just tired, that's all. I did get a set of glasses done, so that's good." Her lips twisted in a lopsided smile. "Four lovely, pregnant goblets. Everything I make these days is round."

"Why don't you go take a nap? Women who are pregnant are supposed to take care of themselves." She rubbed Kate's arms lightly.

"I think I will do that. I want to be rested for class tonight." She rose, steadying herself a bit with Molly's help.

Kate hadn't realized pregnancy would make her so ungainly. With the baby sticking out in front, her center of balance was completely off. Nor had she expected the pregnancy to last forever. She wondered if she would ever have the baby.

"Steve called the shop earlier," Molly said. "He asked me about tonight."

With a sigh, Kate adjusted the controls on the annealing oven and tidied up the workbench. "I'll call him later."

"He wants to come with us."

"I'm supposed to be learning how to relax in class. And leaning on my coach the whole time?" Kate shook her head. "How relaxed can I be with a man who's afraid I'll go into premature labor if he touches me the wrong way?"

Molly laughed. "You have a point there. No Steve this time. Just you and me and baby makes three."

Kate nodded and pulled the bandanna from her head. She kissed Molly on the cheek and left the studio at a slow waddle. The September air felt cool and wonderful after the heat of the crucible. Kate was limp and wrung out. She had pushed herself too hard today. But in the studio she only thought about her art. Anywhere else, she was too prone to brooding about the baby and Steve.

And Patrick.

She sighed and opened the door to her house. If only she could be as certain as she had been the first three months. That clarity of right and wrong seemed so distant and blurred now. She ambled into the bathroom. There, she stripped off her clothes and climbed into the shower. The wet heat felt good against her lower back, which seemed to ache constantly.

With the water pounding on her skin, Kate tried to wash away the loneliness that had crept into her soul. Even with Molly next door and Steve around in the evenings, she still felt alone. In the middle of the night, when she wanted to be held, there was no one there. As much as it pained her to admit it, there was only one person she wanted with her at those moments. Pushing the thought aside, Kate snapped off the shower faucet and grabbed a towel.

After drying herself, she slipped into a loose, light gown and climbed into bed, lying on her side with a pillow for support. Running a hand over her belly, she could feel the kicks and jabs of her baby. She closed her eyes against the stab of tears that threatened. Childbirth class started tonight. The end was in sight, she told herself. Then everything would be better. Everything. She imagined it was true and eventually spiraled down into sleep.

Patrick watched as Kate walked across the alley to her house. She moved slowly with one hand on her lower back. The blue shirt she wore belled out over her stomach, swaying in time to her steps. He almost ducked down in his front seat, but she disappeared into the house without glancing his way. She looked tired, he thought.

He wondered what it felt like now, that bulge of her belly. He remembered touching her, smoothing a hand over the warm, taut skin. Would he be able to feel the baby move if he pressed against her now? Patrick lowered his head to rest on his hands where they gripped the steering wheel. He had missed too much.

When he was certain Kate was safely out of the way in her house, he slipped out of his truck and walked to the studio. Molly wasn't hunched over a potter's wheel this time, but stood with a paintbrush in one hand by a waist-high worktable. Before her was a light brown pot on a stand that rotated. She dabbed pale blue paint onto the pot, slashing and swirling the brush as it turned. He cleared his throat.

"Hello, Molly."

"Patrick! How's the seafarer faring?"

"I—" He paused. "I did what you asked. I stayed away from Kate. I've spent the past five weeks delivering a boat so she could have the time you said she needed." He shoved his hands into his pockets and hunched his shoulders. "But being apart from her is killing me."

"Good. So you want to know if she's ready to see you again?"

"Something like that. And to ask for help."

Her eyes narrowed slightly. "From me?"

Patrick walked over to the bench where she was working. "Please, Molly. You have to convince her to give me another chance. Whether she realizes it or not, Kate needs me." He met the older woman's level stare, swallowing hard. He had to force the next few words out, as if they were wrenched from his soul. "And I need her," he said softly. "I didn't realize how much until I went away."

Molly set down her brush and wiped her hands on a rag. She screwed the cap on the jar of paint, keeping her eyes on the task. Patrick waited, holding on to his patience with both hands.

"Steve's still in the picture." Molly looked over at him briefly, her eyes narrowed.

Patrick drew in a sharp breath, then nodded once. "Okay." The information was a blow, but one he could deal with. If he had the chance.

"Kate starts birthing class tonight," she said, eyes on her task again. "I'm supposed to be her coach."

"Why isn't Steve doing that?"

"You'll have to ask Kate the answer to that question." Molly turned and surveyed him. Her face was solemn, almost stern. "If I let you substitute for me, you have to promise me—" she looked in his eyes and stabbed a finger at his chest "—*promise me* that you will be there for every session. No mistakes and no excuses this time."

Patrick felt his heart lift. Here was not just one chance with Kate, but a whole series of them. "I promise, Molly. Kate comes first, no matter what."

Molly eyed him soberly. "She won't be happy about you taking my place."

Patrick grinned, his delight refusing to subside. "I won't tell her if you don't."

THREE HOURS LATER, Patrick waited impatiently as one couple after another walked through the glass doors into the vestibule. His earlier glee had diminished to anxious anticipation. He tried to smile at the people who glanced his way, but he didn't think he looked very cheerful. He suspected he looked like what he was—a nervous father. He reasoned with himself: *When she sees me, what's the worst she could do? Tell me to get lost? Loudly. While throwing things at me.*

The doors opened again and Patrick caught sight of Kate. When she spotted him, instead of launching an immediate attack, she froze, halfway inside the door, her face a shocked blank. Patrick realized that the worst imaginable wasn't a tantrum; it was no reaction at all.

He stepped toward her just as Molly, carrying a large bag, bumped Kate from behind. Kate stumbled on the floor mat. He rushed forward to stop her fall. She landed against him heavily, her sweet scent enveloping him in roses. It was all he could do to not bury his face in her hair and drink in that aroma. Steadying her against his body, he felt a thump where her belly rested against his. Surprised to feel the baby kick so powerfully, he looked at Kate, his eyes wide. Her hard stare softened slightly.

"Oh, I'm sorry!" Molly's apology seemed to come from far away. "Are you all right, Kate? You stopped so quickly."

Trapped in Kate's chocolate-brown eyes, Patrick echoed Molly's question. "Are you all right, Katie?"

He brushed a lock of her hair behind one ear. He couldn't stop himself from trailing his fingers down her cheek, just to feel the soft skin and touch her any way he could. The caress seemed to jolt Kate out of her stasis. She jerked back. Patrick steadied her gently, then dropped his hands to his side.

"What are you doing here?" Her voice was high and tense as a flush rose to her cheeks.

"I want to be your birthing coach."

She slowly shook her head. "No. That's not possible."

"Sure it is," Patrick said softly. "If you let me, Katie. Please."

"I think the man's right," Molly said. "You should let him do it."

Patrick watched Kate turn an astonished face toward her aunt. "What? Whose side are you on?"

"He's the father of your child, dear. Like it or not, he's the best man for the job."

Kate looked first at her aunt, then at Patrick. He couldn't read anything from her face. Kate had rejected Steve's presence. Why would she welcome him instead?

"Why not give him another chance?" Molly asked. "For the baby's sake."

"But I—"

"Please, Kate," he added quietly. "It's *our* baby."

After a long, tense moment, she nodded once. "All right."

Molly handed Patrick her burden. "Here are the two pillows they told us to bring. You'll deliver her home afterward, won't you?"

Patrick nodded. His heart was pounding and his head felt light. He felt as if he had won the first leg of the most important race of his life. Molly kissed Kate on the cheek, turned and left.

Patrick took Kate's arm. "Come on. I think we're meeting in that room over there."

A woman in a long green dress stepped out of the classroom and looked down the corridor. "Are you part of my birthing class?" she asked with a warm and welcoming smile. "Please come in and find a seat. We're ready to start."

Patrick pulled gently on Kate's hand and led her into the room. They took their places on the remaining two chairs drawn into a circle. The instructor, Marla, greeted them first by introducing herself and listing her qualifications. Then she asked each couple to introduce themselves and tell the group when their child was due and what they liked most about being pregnant.

When their turn came, Patrick let Kate do most of the talking. He was more interested than anyone else in hearing how she was getting along. Kate mentioned how much she loved eating ice cream and talking to her baby when she was by herself. Patrick introduced himself, then quickly told the group that he liked to feel how the baby kicked and squirmed when he touched Kate's stomach.

Next, Marla showed them a video on childbirth and preparing for the trip to the hospital. After that, she called a brief recess and invited everyone to have something to eat and drink at the back of the room. Patrick stuck close to Kate's side, getting her a cup of iced tea and filling a plate with homemade oatmeal cookies for them to eat.

"How are you feeling these days?" Patrick asked casually, careful to preserve the fragile peace between them.

"Fine. Tired."

"The baby's okay, too?"

"Yes." Kate sipped her tea. She darted a look at him.

Patrick held back a sigh. He told himself that her monosyllabic replies were better than no answer at all and curbed his impulse to press her for more. It was not easy after five weeks. He hadn't lied when he said he liked to feel the baby kick. Once was definitely not enough. It was all he could do not to ask Kate if he could put his hands on her belly and feel that thump of life again. They stood awkwardly together, not saying any more until Marla reconvened the class and they returned to their chairs. Their instructor began the second half of class by explaining what life in the womb was like for the baby.

"It's not dark in there, you know," Marla said. "When you see the sonogram, you often get the idea that it's pitch-black inside. There's really more of a rosy glow. Remember putting a flashlight behind your hand when you were a kid and seeing all the veins as dark lines while your hand was bright pink? Well, it's a bit like that for the little one inside the mama. Light filters through your skin.

The baby can even see the shadow of your hand as you press it to your stomach."

Patrick looked at Kate and found the same look of delight on her face that he felt. It was a moment of perfect amity between them. He felt a surge of hope. Marla talked for a few minutes about what to expect in the coming weeks of the class. She asked for questions and, when those were answered, clapped her hands together.

"All right," she said. "Let's move those chairs out of the way. We're going to practice some relaxation techniques before we call it a night. Guys, I want you on the floor first, with Mom propped up against you. Use those pillows to make it comfy."

KATE PUT HER HAND in Patrick's and he supported her as she lowered herself to the floor. Despite the awkwardness of the situation, she couldn't help her snort of laughter. She felt as graceful as a drunken elephant.

"What?" Patrick asked.

"You're going to need a crane to get me up again."

His eyes twinkled and he got down on his knees behind her. "No problem. I know where I can get a twenty-ton travel lift."

Kate kept herself still as he moved to sit down so that she was between his jeans-clad legs. Her hands curled under her chin as she tried not to touch him. Patrick put one of the pillows between them and urged her to recline. She eased back a few inches, then stopped. His hands on her shoulders, he leaned forward.

"It's a relaxation exercise, Katie," he said, his breath puffing in her ear. A shiver went down her spine. "You remember how to relax don't you?"

Marla came by at that moment. "Settle back against him, Mom. He's going to be your prop throughout this whole exercise. When the time comes to do this for real, you'll want this position to be second nature."

Slowly, Kate leaned into Patrick's body. His chin brushed her temple as he adjusted her against his chest. She dropped her hands and laid them lightly on his knees. His scent enveloped her and she closed her eyes to savor the aroma. This felt too right, too good and she stiffened again. Patrick ran his hands over her arms.

"Just lean back." His voice was a low rumble. "I've got you."

Marla led them through the relaxation techniques and guided visualization. The more she said, the easier it became to let go and lean into Patrick. How he had ended up as her coach and whether that was good or bad could be examined another night. Now, she would relax.

She closed her eyes to better absorb the instruction. Breathing deeply, she pulled in more of Patrick's unique scent. She could feel his slow inhale and exhale matching hers. Cares and worries washed away as she leaned against him. Gradually, she felt surrounded, comfortable and safe. She let her mind wander. Marla's voice faded. This was what she had longed for in the night, when she woke alone. This feeling of love and support. Kate knew it was an illusion, but she basked in it anyway.

Patrick smoothed her hair away from her face. "Not falling asleep, are you?"

She could hear gentle humor laced through his words. "Mmm. I could."

Just then, Marla called an end to the class. Kate kept her eyes shut a few moments longer, then roused herself. As she struggled to sit up, Patrick's strong hands pushed her upright. When she was steady he stood, holding out his hands. Taking them, she eased onto her knees and let him haul her up in a breathless swoop.

Kate avoided his eyes as she gathered her things. Marla handed them a booklet and reminded them that next time they would be visiting a birthing center. Patrick was silent as they filed out of the room, lugging the bag of pillows. He held the door for her and walked beside her to his truck.

He opened the door and tossed the pillows into the cab. "You need help climbing in?"

"I don't think so." She put one foot on the step and her hand automatically found the handle on the ceiling, just inside the door. She boosted herself up and in with a laugh.

"Sorry," he said. "I didn't think of how hard it would be to get into the cab."

"It'll be easy to get out of, anyway," Kate said. "That's the trouble with cars. I can get in easily, but I need help to get out of them."

Patrick smiled at that and pulled out the seat belt for her, watching as she snapped it around her girth. When she was settled, he closed the door and went around to the driver's side. He pulled out of the parking lot and headed toward Kate's house. They were silent on the drive. Questions flitted in and out of Kate's head, but none of them seemed to be the right ones to ask. Why had he come to the birthing class? How had he convinced Molly to swap places? They had obviously planned this together. What did he hope to gain? The questions all seemed too combative. The last thing Kate wanted right now was a fight. Instead, she said nothing at all.

At her house, Patrick slid out first then helped her to the ground. He walked beside her to her front door.

"I'll see you next week," he said.

The porch light cast odd shadows over his features so she couldn't read his expression. His voice was neutral, too, giving her no clues. Finally, she nodded.

"Okay."

Patrick hesitated, his arm still at her side supporting her.

"I replaced my cell phone, but the number's the same. Call me anytime you want something."

Kate nodded again. "Thanks. I'll call. If I need you."

"We could practice those relaxation techniques tomorrow or Thursday."

He sounded so earnest, she couldn't help smiling. She turned and unlocked her door. "I'll keep that in mind. Good night, Patrick."

She pushed the door open and went inside as Patrick backed away a step, then turned and trotted down the stairs. She heard him drive away. Her mind whirled with thoughts and doubts. She put her bag down and slowly went to her bedroom. It was only nine-thirty, but she was too tired to stay up any longer.

In bed, she turned out the light and arranged herself into a comfortable position. It was getting harder and harder to do. Settled, she closed her eyes and sighed. She tried to puzzle out her own reactions to the night's events. She should be angry because Patrick had once again thrown her plans into turmoil. She should be angry with Molly for abetting him. She should be angry that, in a weak moment, she had agreed to let him coach her. She should be angry about a whole lot of things, but she wasn't.

What she felt most was a tenuous sort of peace. She held on to it and let everything else fade away. That peace was enough for now. Tomorrow would take care of itself.

Chapter Eleven

Kate felt more and more lethargic with each passing day. In October, a month after the first birthing class, she stopped blowing glass. It was too difficult to do any large pieces and being on her feet wore her out. Instead, she sat on a stool and worked with her bench torch making pendants, brooches and dream catchers. She also spent more time in the shop chatting with customers and, when it was quiet, sketching designs for future work. Friends and acquaintances came in and asked for updates about her baby. Kate answered reassuringly without telling anyone how ready she was to *not* be pregnant.

Childbirth classes progressed, as well. The trip to the birthing center at a local hospital had been interesting and informative, but frightening, too. Seeing the shining sterile equipment—even though it was camouflaged by soft draperies—fed Kate's slow-growing nervousness about actually having the baby. Patrick had worked to calm her, but the worry persisted.

Marla taught them more breathing techniques, turning the room into a giant steam engine with their synchronous huffing and puffing. She introduced birthing balls to get them used to the props they could use during labor. Kate had also borrowed a book from her about water-method birthing, an idea Patrick loved. They filled the drives to class discussing the merits and drawbacks. Patrick's keen interest and participation made Kate deeply happy.

The unhappy one was Steve.

When he learned that Patrick was her coach, it precipitated their first fight. He demanded to know why she had selected Patrick over himself. None of her answers satisfied him. He was especially infuriated when she claimed that it was Patrick's right as the biological father. Steve argued that the man had no rights unless Kate granted them. Patrick was supposed to remain on the sidelines, not take the field with the first string.

Kate couldn't bring herself to do the one thing that would make Steve happy. Even though she knew he was right, she needed Patrick. He alone seemed to know intuitively how to keep her spirits up, no matter how fat and tired she felt. When she obsessed about the baby's health, he had a way of reassuring her that quieted her anxious jitters. The connection between them drove Steve crazy.

Finally, Kate had called a halt. "I won't push Patrick out of my life yet," she said to Steve one evening over dinner. "And if I do, it will be because *I* want him gone, not you." She shook her head and laid down her fork. "Steve, I want to call this off."

"Call what off?" His eyes were wide with alarm.

"You and I trying to be a couple. A family."

"But—"

"It was wrong from the start. I should have known that we would have trouble," she said quietly. "It's my fault. I'm sorry I misled you for all these weeks."

Steve frowned. "So it's over, just like that? Don't I get any say in this?"

"No, you don't." Kate softened her words with a smile. "I'm sorry," she said again.

Steve had pressed his case vehemently, but Kate was firm. In the end, he had stalked out of the restaurant, furious with her. Kate took a cab home, cried a little and felt a wave of relief wash over her. The encounter, painful though it had been, freed her. The tension of having Steve's disapproving presence hovering over her every decision disappeared like smoke.

Despite her relief, being with Patrick didn't get any easier. Their weekly classes were heaven and hell for Kate. It was heaven to be held in Patrick's arms as they practiced breathing exercises or did guided visualizations together. His strong hands stroked and soothed her, rubbing her back in the exact spot where it ached the most. He teased her about being as big as one of his racing boats and threatened to have the crane from the yard brought in to hoist her up at the end of each session. He made her laugh and released her, if only for a short while, from the weary business of being pregnant.

Hell started when she went home after their meetings.

She was sleeping fitfully now, her nights broken by trying to find a comfortable position in bed and frequent trips to the bathroom. The loneliness she had felt before deepened as she lay awake in the darkest hours. She spent too much time thinking about what it would be like to have Patrick beside her.

One Thursday afternoon, she sat in the shop stringing a green and black glass pendant on a silver chain. Patrick was on her mind, as usual. She knew she needed to talk to him about the future, about his role in her and the baby's life, but she couldn't bring herself to broach the subject. She hadn't even told him about breaking up with Steve. He never asked about the other man, or what her plans were. In fact, she had no idea *what* Patrick thought about the future. When she was being honest, Kate admitted that she was afraid to ask.

Though she knew it was a coward's ploy, Kate opted to focus on the baby's arrival and let everything else ride. She was tired and lethargic; all she could think about was the day the baby would arrive. Everything else could wait. She was holding the pendant up to the light, letting the refraction of light hypnotize her, when the bell over the shop door rang. She lifted her head and smiled automatically, putting on her best face for a potential customer. But it was Patrick who stepped through the door, closing it behind him with a bang.

"Hey, Katie. How are you?"

"Hi. I didn't expect to see you today."

He wove his way through the tables of glass and pottery, charmingly displayed to tempt any customers who wandered through. Sturdy plates and bowls stood side by side with delicate glasses in lustrous blue, green and amber. Fanciful clay animals and figurines frolicked at the bases of dramatic vases and fluted bowls in deep emerald and jade. He kept his eyes on her, not sparing a glance for any of it.

Kate felt the feminine thrill of being the focus of this handsome man. Strange and wonderful how Patrick could still make her feel like a woman when, these days, she felt like a hippopotamus.

"Are you here alone?" he asked.

"Shelly's due back at one." Kate looked at her watch: twelve-fifty. "Why?"

"I want you to come look at something with me." Patrick leaned against the counter and ran his eyes over her. He had on a dark blue polar-fleece jacket that gave his gray eyes a touch of color. "You look tired."

"I am. I'm tired of being pregnant." Kate bit her lip. "Sorry. I don't mean to snap."

Patrick grinned. "Someone got up on the wrong side of the bed this morning."

"Several times."

"The kid's not sleeping either, huh?"

Kate sighed. "Not too well. I hope she does better when she's out of there." She laughed a little and rested a hand on her belly. "Maybe she's just getting me ready for all those middle-of-the-night feedings."

"Your own built-in, personal trainer."

They chuckled together at the thought. "What do you want to show me?" she asked.

"Can't tell you. It's a surprise." Patrick held up a hand to stop her before she could speak. "I promise that it's on dry land. I think you'll like it."

Shelly breezed through the door at that moment with a smile. "Brrr! It definitely feels like fall out there today. Hey, Patrick."

"Can you manage this place by yourself for a while?" he asked, before Kate could speak.

"Sure, I usually do. Get Kate out of here. She needs some new scenery."

"Thanks for planning my afternoon for me," Kate said with a cool glance at them both.

Neither appeared the least bothered by her irritation as they grinned at her.

"Get your jacket," Patrick said.

Kate considered arguing, but she decided Shelly was right. She had been staying very close to home over the past weeks. Class with Patrick was just about the only time she got away. An afternoon outing might provide some release from her low spirits. She retreated to the small office behind the counter for her purse. She took a moment to run a comb through her hair and straighten her blouse. Pulling a tube of pink lipstick out of her purse, she paused before applying it.

In the mirror, she could see that she did look tired.

Lipstick wasn't going to cover the fact that she looked fat, either. She dashed on a swath anyway. Taking down a large wool shawl from a hook behind the door, she went out and rejoined Patrick.

"Ready?" he asked, holding out his hand as soon as he saw her.

"Since I don't know where I'm going, I don't know when I'll be back," she told Shelly.

The other woman giggled. "Don't worry about it. I'll lock up when I leave."

Patrick led Kate to his truck and boosted her inside. He drove them to the south of town along the edge of the Bay. Instead of asking again where they were headed, Kate just enjoyed the ride. The first trees were turning color, getting ready for their final burst of glory in a month or so. Ten minutes later, Patrick pulled up in front of a two-story brick house on a quiet street. He got out and came around the truck to help Kate, then took her hand to lead her up the front walk.

The yard was tidy. Burgundy and bright gold chrysanthemums were blooming in the flower beds on either side of the covered front porch. The porch itself was delightful, wide and deep, just perfect for a swing or rocking chairs. At the door, Patrick produced a key and unlocked it.

"Whose house is this?" Kate asked.

"Come take a look." He urged her inside with one hand at her back.

Inside, the house had a traditional layout. The living room was to the left of the front door, the dining room on the right, with a door into what must be a kitchen in the far corner. It was completely empty of furniture. Kate walked a few steps across the oak floor, into the living room and looked around. High ceilings and windows across the front made the room light and spacious. A fireplace was cut into the far wall, with built-in bookcases on either side.

"Nice. Is it for sale?" she asked, turning to look at him.

He stood in the doorway, his hands in his jacket pockets. "Not anymore. I bought it."

Kate's eyes widened. She must have heard wrong. "But you live on a boat."

"Not anymore," he repeated, his mouth turned up slightly at one corner. "I sold it the day before yesterday."

"What?" The word was just a whisper.

"The boat was fine, when there was just me to think about. Now I need more room." He looked down at his shoes, then back at her. His face—his eyes—were unreadable. "There's a room upstairs that would be perfect for a nursery. Do you want to take a look?" He made a vague gesture toward the stairs, but didn't take his gaze off her.

Kate swallowed hard. "Patrick, I—"

"I'm not expecting anything," he said, interrupting her. "I'm just letting you know that I can change. That I *want* to. Sailing has been my life, but it doesn't have to be the *only* thing in my life."

Her eyes filled with tears and she closed them tightly. She felt emotionally blindsided and completely befuddled. When she opened her eyes, Patrick had moved closer. He held out a hand.

"Come look at the rest of it, Katie. I want to know what you think."

Searching his face, she only saw calm assurance. "I don't know what this means, Patrick." The words were almost a plea.

He stroked her cheek. "It's only a tour of my new house." He enfolded her hand in his with a strong, steady grip. "You can tell me what furniture to buy. Otherwise I'll just fill it up with sails and boat gear." With a tug, he had her following him across the floor to the stairs. "There's even a view of the Bay, if you stand on the toilet seat."

"SEE, I TOLD YOU she'd love it," Evan said.

"I wouldn't say that. She was pretty quiet the whole time we were there."

"Yeah, but she *will* love it. It was a good idea." Evan leaned back against the table saw in Ian's workshop. His immaculately tailored, charcoal suit jacket became dotted with sawdust. "Buying a house was a stroke of genius. I'm surprised you came up with it on your own."

"Yeah, what's with that?" Ian asked. He ran a hand plane lightly over a piece of teak clamped in a vise. Paper-thin shavings of wood littered the edge of the table and the floor. "If you're not careful, somebody might mistake you for a grown-up."

"Screw you both," Patrick said with a smile. He played with a scrap of wood, turning it over and over in his hands. Thinking about the afternoon with Kate, he frowned. "I don't know. Maybe I put too much pressure on her."

"Why would she feel pressured?" Evan asked, his tone dry and one blond eyebrow arched.

Ian chuckled, keeping his eyes on his work. "The guy she thinks is a boat bum just sold his boat and bought a house. With a nursery." He shook his head. "Nope, no pressure at all."

Evan laughed and Patrick tossed the block of wood at him. His phone rang before he could make any rude remarks. He flipped it open and saw the name and number. "Chris! How's it going, man?"

"Not so great." Chris paused. "There's no good way to

tell you this, so I'm just gonna say it. Greg got swept off *Vertex*, Patrick. He's dead."

"What?" Patrick's delight disappeared in an instant. "When?"

"Day before yesterday."

Patrick closed his eyes, as if blocking out sight would shut out reality. Pressing a thumb and forefinger into his eyes, he held back the stinging tears that threatened. "How'd it happen?"

"A squall popped up. They got hit hard with winds and waves and Greg went over the stern. I don't know why he wasn't clipped in. The tactician saw him fall, but he was gone before anyone could grab him." Chris's voice choked to a halt. He cleared his throat. "They recovered his body. They think he was probably dead when he hit the water. He must have struck his head on something."

"Oh, my God." Patrick shivered to think of it.

"We need you, man," Chris said, bringing Patrick's attention back to the phone call. "You have to come skipper the boat."

"Whoa, Chris. I'm going to have to think about that."

"Think fast, then. I want you here yesterday." Chris sighed. "Everybody's slayed over this, Patrick. It's like we're all wandering around in a fog or something. Total chaos, too. Greg held us all together, y'know? Without him…" Chris trailed off and there was a silence on the phone. "We *need* you, man. You're the only one who can take over for him."

"That's not—"

"It *is*, Patrick. With you at the helm, I know we can win this thing."

"I'll…I'll have to call you back later," Patrick said. His mind was reeling, trying to take in all the things his friend was saying. "I...I don't know what else to say, Chris. Tell Stacy...tell her how sorry I am, please. And everyone on the crew."

"I will, but I'd rather tell them you're on your way to win this one for Greg."

"I'll think about it and give you a call," Patrick repeated. "Bye." He closed the phone and stared at it.

"What was that about?" Ian asked.

"Greg Chastain was swept off *Vertex Commander.*"

"Oh, shit. Where?"

"I don't know exactly. It must have been this side of Australia."

"Is he—" Ian didn't finish the question.

Patrick took a breath as a sharp stab of grief hit him. He dropped the phone back in his pocket before bracing his hands against the workbench. His head drooped between his shoulder blades for a long moment. He couldn't speak the two words. They were too painful. If he said them aloud they would become true—the last thing he wanted—but silence would not change the reality. He raised his head and looked at his brother.

"He's dead."

Ian put the plane down and walked around to Patrick's side of the table. He pulled his brother into his arms. They held on tight to each other for a long minute, while Evan gripped Patrick's shoulder. Patrick pulled back, wiping away tears and taking a deep breath.

Ian gripped Patrick's biceps. "You going to be okay?"

Patrick nodded halfheartedly. "He was a good friend."

"What happened?" Evan asked.

Patrick repeated what Chris had told him.

"What the hell was he thinking, not clipping in?" Evan asked with a frown.

Patrick shook his head. "I don't know. If the weather

was good, he might not have bothered. Sometimes you don't, you know. It depends on how the ship's run."

"Still—"

"He was the skipper. It was his call."

The three men were silent. "Well, I'm sorry, man," Evan said. "Did he have family?"

"A girlfriend. Stacy. I met her in France last time I was there." Patrick thought about the shy, sweet woman with Greg on the docks. She must be devastated.

"Come on. Let's get out of here," Ian said.

They grabbed their jackets and headed out of the workshop, across the parking lot. Once away from of the yard, they walked down the street to a small waterside bar just past the marina. The bartender called a greeting. Ian ordered three beers. Evan led the way to a table in the back, overlooking the water. Immediately after they sat, a waitress in tight blue jeans and dyed-blond hair plunked three pint glasses on the table.

When she left, Patrick raised his glass in a silent toast for his friend. After they drank, Patrick said, "There was a second reason that Chris called me."

"What other reason could he have?" Evan asked, eyebrows raised.

Patrick turned his glass on the table, then looked at his brother and his friend. "They want me to take Greg's place and skipper the boat for the rest of the race."

"You're kidding!" Evan's eyes lit at the news. "That's fantastic."

"I haven't told them whether I'd do it or not."

"Of course you'll do it," Evan said. "The next leg is through the Indian Ocean. What a ride!"

"It would be a great sail." Patrick smiled at his friend's vicarious glee. For a minute, grief was pushed aside.

Evan leaned forward. "Can you bring a friend?"

"I doubt it."

"What about Kate?" Ian asked.

Patrick took another sip of his beer. "She's my reason for hesitating."

"But it's the Globe Challenge. The big one. The one you've always dreamed about," Evan reminded him. "You can't say no."

"Sure I can." Patrick looked out the window. "I've done that stretch of ocean before and I will again. That's not the problem."

"So what's the problem?" Ian asked.

"Greg Chastain."

"He's dead."

"Yeah, but I owe him a lot," Patrick said with a sigh, leaning back in his chair. "He gave me my first shot at running a big boat. If it weren't for him I wouldn't be where I am today."

"I doubt that," Evan said. "You're one of the best. He may have given you a start, but you did the rest on your own."

Patrick shrugged the praise away. "Maybe, but I still owe him. Greg had a shot at winning this one. The boat's second in the standings." He looked at his brother. "If I take over, I could finish what he started. I could even win it for him. For his memory."

"But Kate's nearly eight months' pregnant," Ian said, his voice soft.

"Yeah." Patrick sipped his beer. An idea hit him. "She's not due for five weeks, right? There's a layover while they do repairs and get ready for the next leg. I could go over for a couple of weeks, maybe three, then come back and be here for the baby's birth. Afterward, I can go back and skipper the race. It might work out."

"What if the baby comes early? Or late for that matter?" Ian shot a hard glance at his brother. "And, even if the kid pops out right on your schedule, do you want to leave Kate for the rest of the race? You're talking months, Patty."

"But this is important. It's about finishing what Greg started."

"What about finishing what *you* started?" Ian asked.

"I *will* be finishing it." Patrick looked over at his brother impatiently. "Why does everyone think racing and being a father are mutually exclusive?"

"I'm just saying—"

"Look, *you* were the one that said I could do both."

"When did I say that?"

"That day I punched my truck. You said it was reasonable that I could do both."

"That was—" Ian stopped and huffed out a breath. "You talk some sense into him," he said to Evan.

"I say talk to Kate and see what she says, but bottom line, I'd do the race," Evan said. "This is the Globe. It's only run every four years. You'd be skippering the best boat ever to come out of this country. You turn this down and you might not get another shot."

"How often does he get to see his first child born?" Ian asked, slapping his hand on the table.

"It's not going to happen tomorrow," Evan said with a shrug. "I agree with Patrick. Fly over for a couple of weeks, then come back for the kid."

Ian looked back and forth between the two other men. "You guys are both nuts." He turned to Patrick. "You have a chance here, Patty. Don't let it slip away."

"I'm not going to," Patrick said. "Look, when I tell Kate about Greg, she's *got* to understand how important it is that I do this."

Ian shook his head, but was silent. Patrick sat back and lifted his glass. This *was* his opportunity. And also a chance to show Kate how their lives could work around racing. It seemed like a perfect, simple plan. He would be a father and a racer. The best of both worlds.

KATE WAS SURPRISED to hear a knock on her door that evening. She checked the peephole and was more surprised to see Patrick standing there. She felt a rush of the same confusion she had felt earlier. After he had told her that he owned the house, she hadn't known what to say or how to act. He had kept up a commentary about the place, asking her for opinions and advice, mentioning nothing about the future.

Only when they reached one room did he pause. He didn't say it, but she knew they were in the room he had picked as the nursery. It was so bright and cheerful. Kate could easily picture it furnished with a crib and changing table, a rocker in one corner for night feedings.

Now she hesitated, uncertain what other surprise he might have for her this evening. She put a hand on the door knob and clicked open the dead bolt with the other, slowly pulling the door open.

"Hi." The word came out part greeting, part question.

"Can I come in?" he asked.

She frowned and stood aside, closing the door behind him. Looking at him in the better light of the hall, she was alarmed. His eyes were red rimmed and, usually so opaque, tonight they held a wealth of sadness.

"What's wrong?"

He shrugged. "I got some bad news today."

He looked so lost just then that Kate took his arm, urging him into the living room and to a seat on one of the sofas. "Sit down, Patrick." Her voice was gentle and soft. "Tell me what happened."

Patrick sat, propping his elbows on his knees and burying his face in his hands. "A friend of mine died." His voice was muffled but filled with pain.

"Oh!" Kate sucked in a quick breath and laid a hand on his shoulder. She felt it tremble slightly. She sat down and put an arm around him. "How did it happen?"

Patrick scrubbed his hands down his face. "He was racing in the Tasman Sea. He was swept off the boat."

The news made Kate gasp again. Immediately, fear for Patrick flooded through her. "Oh, no."

"It was a freak accident. It should never have happened."

Kate struggled with her composure. The thought of Patrick being lost that way sent her heart into a fast, frightened pulse. She tamped down the anxiety, taking deep breaths, reminding herself that he was here, safe in her living room. Sitting back on the sofa, she focused on Patrick's drawn face. She needed to help him, not let her own fears take over.

Patrick's eyes lost their focus as he told her about the man he had known and admired. "I'll miss him."

"He must have meant a lot to you."

With a nod, Patrick dropped his head against the back of the sofa. They sat in silence for a long time. Wind from a passing squall rattled the windows and blew a splatter of rain across the glass. Eventually, Patrick turned his head to look at Kate.

"Thanks for listening to me ramble."

"I'm glad you came over." Smiling, she reached out and squeezed his hand.

"There wasn't anywhere else I wanted to be," he said softly.

His words brought a flush of pleasure to Kate's heart.

Patrick straightened from his slouched position. Leaning toward her, he ran his fingertips down her cheek lightly. "Can I stay?" he asked, his voice just above a whisper.

Kate looked at him, outwardly calm while a storm

raged inside. Her heart and her head were in sudden and violent battle. *No,* her head raged, *he'll only hurt you again. Yes,* her heart countered with a sigh, *all these lonely nights, he's the one you missed.*

"Please. I don't want to be alone tonight."

His eyes pleaded with her, dark gray and sad. Kate found herself nodding her head. Patrick's look of relief and gratitude swept her doubts away. He rose to his feet and drew her upward. With their arms around each other, they went into the bedroom. There were no words spoken as they prepared for bed, first one using the bathroom, then the other.

Kate smiled at herself in the mirror as she dried her face. She couldn't feel less sexy tonight and she doubted her bloated body would hold any appeal for Patrick. How different this was than the last time he had shared her bed. He was under the covers when she returned to the bedroom. She climbed in beside him, laughing a little at her gracelessness.

"Sorry. It's going to be a little like sleeping with an elephant tonight."

Patrick chuckled. "I'll manage, Mrs. Jumbo."

The *Dumbo* reference made her giggle. She turned off the bedside light, then arranged herself on her right side, facing away from Patrick. Without speaking, he tucked himself against her back. It was similar to birthing class, but they were lying on their sides. He slipped one arm under her neck, below her pillow. With the other hand, he urged her to lean into his chest. The support of his strong body was much better than the mound of pillows she normally used. When he rubbed her back she nearly groaned aloud.

"Where have you been all my life," she said on a moan of pleasure-pain from his ministrations.

"Now I know why you let me stay the night."

"You have to earn your keep." Kate sighed and relaxed into him even further. Patrick nuzzled his face into her hair and fell silent. He stopped his massage and his hand slid over her belly. The baby kicked once against his touch, then twice. His fingers spread over her. Slowly, as if waiting for her to protest, he pulled at her gown until he could reach the bare skin of her stomach.

His touch was electrifying and Kate gave a little cry of shock, quickly smothered. Patrick made a humming noise in her ear, low and hoarse. The arm under her neck curled around to cross her chest and cup one of her breasts in his palm. It tightened in response to his touch and she moaned as he circled the nipple with his thumb. Meanwhile, he explored her pregnancy with his other hand, smoothing and teasing her skin. As his hand slipped lower to find the sensitive spot between her legs, Kate grabbed his arm.

"No, Patrick."

"Does it hurt?"

"No, I just—"

"Then let me touch you, Katie," he said softly. His breath in her ear made her shiver. "You're so beautiful."

"I'm nearly eight months' pregnant. That is *not* beautiful."

He laughed softly. "If you only knew." He paused and Kate held her breath, waiting. "When we're in class together and you're in my arms, I want time to stop and all those other people to disappear." Patrick's voice dropped to a whisper. "I want to touch you all I can, Katie. You're carrying my child. *Mine.* I think you're gorgeous."

Kate's heart filled her throat and she couldn't speak. He gently twisted his wrist free of her grasp and sought the delicate bud between her legs once more. She gasped and sighed at the touch of his callused fingers. He knew exactly how much pressure to exert, where to press and when to tease. She felt him grow hard against her and reached a hand back to caress him. He stopped his pleasuring of her to take her hand and raise it to his lips.

"This is for you. Not me."

"But I want you, Patrick," she said in a whisper of need. "Please."

"I don't want to hurt the baby." He kissed the back of her neck.

"You won't. I promise."

He let her hand stroke him, his breath fast and hot in her ear. When he moved away, she released him. He drew her leg up and over his as he positioned himself and slid slowly inside her from behind. As he thrust carefully, his fingers returned to their tantalizing forays. Slowly, he built her pleasure until she was writhing in his arms, desperate for release. She moaned and begged him to finish what he had started. Patrick complied, pressing himself deep within her and using his thumb to send her over the edge of ecstasy. Kate cried out, feeling the tingle spread to every nerve ending. His muffled shout of pleasure joined hers seconds later. She panted and a laugh came to her lips.

"Oh, my Patrick," she said on a sigh.

He clasped his arms around her, pressing a kiss to the side of her neck. Kate put her hand up and slipped her fingers into his thick hair, holding his head against her. Sleep claimed her quickly, though, and she fell, relaxed and content in his arms. Tonight she would not be lonely.

Chapter Twelve

Kate woke when sunshine spread across the room and hit her face. She opened her eyes and knew she was alone in bed. A sense of déjà vu swept through her and she looked toward the bathroom, expecting Patrick to come through the door. He didn't, but it didn't upset her. She had slept too well to let his desertion throw her. He might be gone, but he had given her one of the best nights of her life.

She levered herself up and began the slow process of getting out of bed and to the bathroom. It had been much easier in the night with Patrick's assistance. She smiled as she splashed water on her face and ran a brush through her hair. Even the fact that her bathrobe barely closed around her girth didn't ripple her pleasure.

Shuffling down the hall, Kate heard voices coming from the kitchen. When she reached the doorway, her mouth dropped open in astonishment. Patrick and Molly sat on either side of the table, coffee cups on the table before them. A newspaper was gutted and scattered over its surface. Molly wagged a finger at Patrick as he looked back at her, a grin on his face.

"That's where you're wrong, young man—"

"Does this mean I get to call you 'old lady' now?"

Molly stiffened and her eyes narrowed. "Only if you have complete disregard for your physical safety."

Patrick threw his head back and laughed. As he did, Molly caught sight of Kate. "There you are," she said. "You're just in time. The muffins will be ready—" The oven timer buzzed. "Right now."

Molly rose and went to the stove. Kate remained where she stood, still shocked. Molly and Patrick had never gotten along. Yet here they were in her kitchen, sharing coffee, muffins, a newspaper and chummy banter. Patrick came over to Kate and drew her into the warm, fragrant kitchen. He pressed a light kiss to her lips and pulled a chair out for her. He winked at her, a warm glow lingering in his eyes. Kate felt a blush creep up her cheeks.

Molly plunked an earthenware mug in front of her. "Herbal tea, for you, my dear. How did you sleep?"

"Fine." Kate said in a strangled voice.

"Like an elephant," Patrick said with a smile, as he sat diagonally across the table from her. He grinned again at Molly, who stood with raised brows. "Lumbers around a lot, snores like a freight train."

"I do not!"

"Molly, guess how many times an elephant goes to the bathroom at night." Patrick's eyes twinkled with his teasing.

"You didn't have to stay." Kate sipped her tea.

Patrick ran a finger down her cheek. The look in his eyes had her blushing anew as she remembered his touch the night before. "Yeah, Katie, I did."

Molly glanced at them, a smile on her face. Patrick laced his fingers with Kate's and held her gaze with his. A shadow passed through his eyes, turning them dark.

"And thank you for letting me stay." His voice was low, meant for her ears only. "I needed to hold you last night."

"How do you feel?"

Patrick took a deep breath. "Better. Thanks to you."

A warm feeling swept over Kate. She squeezed his fingers and Patrick sat back as Molly put a basket of steaming muffins on the table. She handed out plates and silverware, then placed butter and honey alongside the basket. After refilling the two cups with coffee, Molly sat and they dived into breakfast.

"Patrick's going to take you to your doctor's appointment this morning," her aunt announced, liberally smearing butter on half of a muffin. "I've got a meeting with a woman who wants me to do an entire set of dishes to match her wallpaper."

"That's crazy," Kate said, incredulous.

Molly shrugged. "Maybe, but, for the price of a service for twelve, I'll indulge the dingbat."

"See if you can talk her into glassware to match the drapes, why don't you? If she's going to throw away money, she might as well throw it at me, too."

Molly laughed. "I'm sure I could easily convince her. She loved your stuff in the shop yesterday. I told her you couldn't meet her this morning, but she may want to see you when she gets back from her trip. She leaves for Italy this afternoon to look at some furniture."

Kate shook her head and took a muffin from the basket. She cut it in half and added a pat of butter to each side, letting it melt.

"What time do you need to be at the doctor?" Patrick bit into the soft, warm bread. "This is fabulous," he mumbled through crumbs.

"Ten-fifteen." Kate took a bite of the muffin she held and nodded at her aunt. "He's right, these are terrific."

Molly beamed at their compliments. "Pumpkin-spice. I got the recipe from Suzanne at the coffee shop and then tweaked it a little."

Kate bemusedly listened as Patrick and Molly took up their earlier debate about a condo project that was planned for a vacant property nearby. Molly was against the construction and Patrick, though he claimed to be neutral, fanned the flames of Molly's ire with every word he spoke.

"I like tall buildings. You can see them for miles. They're like navigation beacons." Patrick's half-hidden smile and twinkling eyes showed his true sentiment, but the remark reduced Molly to speechlessness. "You should meet Jimmy Johnson sometime," he added. "You might like him. He's got the same opinions you do. And he's no good at arguing, either."

Molly threw her napkin at him and he laughed. Rising, he cleared the table, ordering the women to stay seated. After he cleaned the kitchen, he announced that he was going to shower.

"You two seem pretty chummy this morning," Kate said to her aunt after Patrick left.

"I've gotten to know him better over the past few weeks." Molly leaned her elbows on the table. "I like him. He's not what I thought he was. He's in love with you." Her clear blue eyes caught Kate's in an intense stare.

Kate dropped her own eyes and toyed with the tab from her tea bag, still dangling off the side of her mug. She wanted to believe that, but she was afraid to, afraid of her own wishful thinking. "He sold his boat," she said.

"Really?"

"And bought a house."

Molly's eyes opened wide. "You're *kidding*. Why would he do that?"

"He claims he needs more room."

Her aunt was silent for a while. "Did he ask you to move in with him?"

"Not yet. He hasn't said anything except that there's a

room that would be perfect for a nursery. He's right. It was perfect." Kate smiled as she mentally filled the cozy room with baby furniture.

"You saw it?"

"He took me there yesterday. It's over on Clements, not far from Bayside Park."

Molly sipped her coffee. "Hmm."

Kate laughed at the expression on her face. "That's what I think. Am I deceiving myself, Molly? Has he changed?" She looked at her aunt with pleading eyes. "He's been wonderful as a coach and I, I—" She paused and swallowed back the lump in her throat. "I want him to be different, but I don't trust myself to know if he is or isn't."

"I didn't know him all that well before, so it's hard for me to say. I like him, Katie, but that's not a very informed opinion."

"I like him, too." Kate sighed softly.

"You *love* him, you mean."

Kate shifted in her seat and kept her eyes on her mug. "I don't want to."

Molly put her hand over Kate's and squeezed. "Love isn't something you can control. It's not like molten glass. It's alive, sometimes with a mind of its own."

With a snort, Kate lifted the cup to her lips and drank the last swallow. "I know that. If it behaved itself, I'd be in love with Steve Craig right now and Patrick would be long gone."

Molly smiled. "I can't tell you what to do, sweetheart, but I will give you some advice. Listen to your heart. It often has the best idea of what will make you happy in the long run."

Patrick strode back into the kitchen, smelling like her floral shampoo. It didn't make him any less masculine. In fact, the effect was exactly the opposite. His hair was slicked down, the natural waves tamed and his jaw was smoothly shaved. Kate's heart sped up, thinking about what Molly had said about him being in love with her.

Patrick gathered up the paper, glancing over to see her watching him. He smiled. "Better get a move on, Katie, my love. It's nine-fifteen."

Kate pushed herself from the table and he helped her to her feet. He patted her on the butt as she passed and laughed at the glare she shot at him. As she got ready for her appointment, Kate's thoughts ambled in confusion. Should she give Patrick the chance her heart wanted her to give him? She wished there was a clear answer. If only something would point her in the right direction. All the signs that whirled in her head pointed in every which direction.

"I'M SORRY that took so long. The doctor's usually not so backed up." Kate adjusted the heater to send more hot air into the cab.

"Not much she can do when a baby decides to pop out first thing in the morning." Patrick shifted gears and glanced over at Kate's bulging stomach. "Think you can time it a little better?"

Kate shot him a dry look. "I'll make sure to check with your schedule before going into labor."

Patrick grinned and kept his eyes on the road. "Do you mind if we stop at the marina on our way back to your place? My mother left a message while we were in the doctor's office. She needs me to talk to a customer who's there right now."

"That's fine. I can wait in the truck."

"Could you do me a favor and come into the office? Ma's dying to see you, again. She's been trying to get me to bring you by for weeks." Kate was silent and Patrick knew she was thinking the same thing he was. "She'll be thrilled. Get ready for some serious grandmother action, though."

"Is she into her grandkids?"

"Are you kidding?" Patrick asked with a laugh. "She's Irish. It's all about family for her."

Kate frowned slightly. "I thought your family was Italian."

"On my father's side. My mother's so Irish, she bleeds green."

"And they get along?"

"Yeah. They love each other a lot." Remembering what Kate had said about her parents, Patrick thought again how lucky he was. "Not to say that they haven't had their moments. They both have pretty volatile tempers. Which makes for some interesting fights." He chuckled. "Ian got grounded for a week once, when he asked them if they minded putting an argument on hold so he could make popcorn and enjoy the show."

Kate burst out laughing at that. Patrick turned into the parking lot at the marina and pulled into a slot. He went around to help Kate down and they walked to the office as fast as she was able. The wind was blowing a gale, much fiercer near the water than farther inland. Patrick shielded Kate from the brunt of it until they were inside.

A wide, excited smile lit Elaine's face when she saw Kate. She spoke a few words into the phone she held to her ear, then dropped it with a bang.

"Finally!" Elaine came around the counter and took Kate's hands in hers. "Oh, look at you! You're just beautiful."

Patrick gave Kate an I-told-you-so look and kissed his mother on the cheek. "Nice to see you, too, Ma."

Elaine patted him on the shoulder, but kept her eyes glued to Kate. She drew her over to the empty desk facing her own. "Sit down, dear. Patrick, your father is on the docks with—oh, here they are now."

Antonio Berzani walked into the office followed by a short, squat man with receding brown hair. Both men sported wild, windblown hair and ruddy cheeks.

"Gusting over forty now, I'd say," Antonio said with a laugh. "Katerina!" He came to Kate and pressed a kiss to each of her cheeks, then patted her stomach. "This is a big one, eh? Probably a boy. You name him Antonio, for me, okay? Someone in this family needs a good Italian name!"

Patrick saw Kate flush with color, but Elaine shooed his father away. "Go talk boats and leave us alone."

Antonio pressed a kiss to his wife's lips. "Anything for you, my love."

"Scat!"

Patrick shared a look with Kate, then turned and greeted the other man. "Patrick Berzani," he said, holding out his hand.

The man shook it. "Roger Whited. Nice to meet you."

Antonio stood next to Patrick. "Roger's buying a Harris 60 and may have us do the commissioning. I took him on a tour of the yard, but he wanted to talk to you, too."

"What can I tell you, Mr. Whited?"

"This yard and you, especially, were recommended to me by Greg Chastain. I've had a boat in San Francisco for years and now I want one on this coast, too. He said you were the man for the job."

"I'm glad Greg thought that highly of me." Patrick's voice faltered as he said his friend's name. He swallowed hard, looking away from Mr. Whited and his father.

"Patricio?" Antonio gripped Patrick's shoulder. "What's wrong?"

Patrick cleared his throat. "Mr. Whited, I don't know how—" He took a deep breath and met the man's puzzled stare. "I'm sorry, but talking about Greg is hard right now. I got a call yesterday from a friend on his boat. Greg got swept off in a squall. He's…he's dead."

Roger Whited paled and put a hand out to grip the edge of the counter.

"This is the friend Ian told us about last night?" Antonio asked.

"Yeah," Patrick said, nodding. "I'm sorry to spring it on you, Mr. Whited. I just thought you should know."

"Please, call me Roger." He took a deep breath. "No, no. I'm glad you told me, but it is a shock. You just heard yesterday?"

"It happened in the Tasman Sea. They were two days out, at the most."

"I'm sorry to hear that," Roger said. "Greg was a great guy. A great sailor. I've been following the race when I can."

"Patricio is going to skipper his friend's boat," Antonio said proudly.

"He is?"

Turning around, Patrick saw that Kate was standing at his elbow. She had heard his father's announcement and her face turned pale. The cup of coffee trembled in her hand. He took the cup and put it on the counter to take her hands in his.

"Kate, I—"

"Is it true? You're going to sail that boat?" she asked.

"And win, of course," Antonio said, before Patrick could answer.

"It would be a great sail," Roger said, his eyes alight

with the idea. "And winning would be an amazing way to honor Greg."

"You're taking the place of a *dead* man?" Kate asked in a shaky voice. She slipped her hands away from Patrick's and twisted them together.

"Easy, Kate. I have to do it. Don't you see? For Greg," Patrick said. His heart started to pound at the terrified look in her eyes. "I'll be careful. Greg must have got careless or cocky and he didn't clip in. I won't make the same mistake."

Kate looked at him, her brown eyes nearly black now. "So you say."

"Really—"

"Are you all right, dear?" Elaine asked, coming up and putting a hand on Kate's arm. Her eyes were filled with concern. "Do you want to sit down again?"

"I'm a little tired," Kate said quietly, her eyes averted.

Elaine and Antonio exchanged a look. Roger darted glances at all of them, seeming to catch the tension in the air. He cleared his throat, but Antonio spoke first.

"Patricio, you should take her home. This is no day to be out. Not in her condition. And it's going to get worse. The tropical depression will be right over us soon."

"I'm sorry," Patrick said to Roger Whited. "We'll have to talk about this another time."

"Not a problem," Roger said. He handed Patrick his card. "Call me anytime. I want you to do the work," he added. "Everything your father showed me here is top-notch."

"Thanks Mr., uh, I mean, Roger. I appreciate the business," Patrick said, shaking the other man's hand. He looked over at Kate. She was still pale and her expression guarded. "I'll call you tomorrow."

"That will be fine."

Patrick grabbed Kate's shawl and wrapped it around her shoulders. Elaine kissed her cheek and asked her to come back soon. Out of the office, the wind blew them toward the truck and he had to wrestle the door to get it open. Once inside, he turned to Kate. "Look, I was going to tell you."

"Just take me home, Patrick."

"It's a huge opportunity and an honor to be asked. We have to talk about this."

"Later. I don't feel well right now."

"Is it the baby?"

"It's everything," she said in a miserable tone. She leaned back and closed her eyes. "Please, just take me home."

Patrick could hear tears in her voice. Her words tore at him. Reluctantly, he started the truck and drove to her house. The winds buffeted the vehicle. He fought to keep it on the road. He stole glances at her in the seat next to him, but she never opened her eyes once. A chasm had opened between them. It seemed wider for having the intimacy of last night and this morning so close at hand. He told himself they would work it all out. He had to believe it. The other option was unbearable.

Chapter Thirteen

Kate unclipped her seat belt and let Patrick help her out of the truck. She kept her eyes averted, steeling herself against the words she knew she must say. Walking slowly up the steps, she unlocked the front door, went inside and into the living room. Patrick followed closely.

"Why didn't you tell me about this race?" She took off her shawl and laid it over the back of one of the sofas.

"I was going to, once I had it all worked out."

"Had what all worked out?"

"I thought it through yesterday and last night, Katie," Patrick said, coming to her and putting his hands on her shoulders. "They need me to skipper the boat, but I know I need to be here, too. The way I figure it, it'll work out perfectly. I'll go to Australia for a couple of weeks and get the crew organized for the layover. When they're set, I'll come back and be here for the baby's arrival. Afterward, I'll go back and sail the next leg of the race. When the boat hits port, I'll fly home."

"So, your plan is to abandon me." Tears rose to her eyes and she blinked them away. His words seemed to punch a hole right through her, leaving a gaping wound in her heart and soul.

"No, Katie. I just…I really want to do this race for Greg. I *need* to."

"I need you here, Patrick."

Kate pulled away from his touch, went around the sofa and sat down. She felt tired, cold and lonely once again. Patrick followed and sat facing her, one long leg folded under him.

"It'll only be for a short while," he said urgently. "After the baby's born, I'll be gone for a few weeks at a time, but back for weeks at a time, too."

"Unless you don't come back at all."

Patrick smoothed a hand over her windblown hair, tucking a strand behind her ear. "Of course I'm coming back."

"Just like your friend did?" she asked softly.

Patrick frowned. "How often do you think something like that happens on a boat?"

"I've heard stories about three races, Patrick. In two of them, someone died." Kate tugged at the throw pillow beside her, twisting her fingers into the fringe. "The odds seem pretty atrocious to me."

"That's not going to happen to me."

"How can you be so certain?"

"I just am." Patrick sat forward and pulled the cushion from her, taking her hands in his and squeezing them tightly. "I'm a good sailor, Kate."

"Nobody's that good all the time. You said it yourself, *accidents happen.*"

"Look, it's not going to happen. I'll be careful. I'll clip in, I promise."

Kate slipped her hands away and shifted, sliding to the edge of the sofa. She couldn't sit still any longer. Patrick guessed her intentions and swiftly rose to help her stand up. Tears stung her eyes once again. He was so thoughtful, so understanding of her needs. But there were some needs he would never be able to fill. On her feet, she moved away from him.

"Careful doesn't win races, Patrick. You said that once, too."

"I didn't mean—"

"My brother told me he was careful." Kate rubbed her hands up and down her arms, warming the sudden spate of goose bumps that had risen. "'Don't worry, sis,' he'd say. 'Nothing's going to happen to me.' He was wrong and you are, too."

Patrick came to her side, looking at her intently. "What happened to him?"

"He jumped out of a plane and his parachute didn't open. They don't know why. It was an accident. Just like Greg's."

"I'm sorry, Katie." There was silence between them broken only by the occasional rattle of the windows in a particularly strong gust of wind. "Look, skydiving is different than sailing."

"Is it?" she asked. "My brother jumped out of planes for the same reason that you race on the ocean—he loved the rush."

"I don't go out there trying to kill myself."

Kate laughed humorlessly. "No? Then what is it? You push, Patrick. You push, and you push and *you push*. Anything to win the race."

"Not anything."

"You sailed your boat just *feet* in front of a container ship to get a few extra minutes in a race where winning didn't even matter. In one that did, you almost capsized a boat to get to the finish line first. What do you call that?"

"You're completely wrong, Kate. You've taken two incidents and made up some theory that I go crazy as soon as I set foot on a boat. I don't. How could I and be so successful for so long?"

"I don't know," Kate said, shaking her head. "I don't care, either."

"What does that mean?"

"I don't want you in my life anymore, Patrick."

"What?" His voice dropped to a whisper. "You don't mean that."

"Yes, I do. This baby and I need someone who will be here. You won't change."

She walked to the window and looked out at the blustery day. The tree branches whipped back and forth and rain now sprayed the street in blasts. Kate slid her hands to her belly, rubbing the mound gently, taking comfort from the life that danced and spun inside her.

"There's no compromise for you, is there?" Patrick asked, his voice hard. "I give up racing or I can't be a father to *my* child."

"I'm not asking you to compromise." Tears filled Kate's eyes and she turned to face him. "I'm asking you to put being a father *first*."

"I *am*."

"You've made plans to leave me five weeks before our child will be born, without telling me about it. Then, you're going to leave the minute she's born and risk never coming home again. What kind of father does that?" Kate's voice rose to a shout. The tears she had held in check rose and spilled over her lashes. "I need you to put me and the baby first, but you can't. You won't ever be able to put us first."

"All right! Have it your way. I won't go."

Kate shook her head, wiping the tears from her cheeks with one hand. "It doesn't matter whether you go or not, Patrick. You'll never be a real father to this baby."

"Who will be, then?" he said furiously. "Steve?"

The lie was like a lifeline thrown to her out of a storm. She lunged for it and held on tight. "Yes."

He froze and his face paled beneath his tan. "I thought—" He faltered to a stop. After a long, silent moment, in a low voice, he asked, "You're going to marry him? Even after last night?"

Kate nodded.

"So, I suppose I should go to Australia. Get on the boat and finish the race for Greg."

Kate bit her lip on the cry that rose in her throat. The thought of him leaving, putting himself in danger, chilled her to the bone, yet she held back her plea for him to stay. She had no right to ask anything of him. Her silence was his only answer.

Patrick looked at her for a long moment, waiting for more, his eyes tracing each of her features as if memorizing them. When she said nothing, he turned and walked out of the room. The front door closed quietly behind him. The silent exit wounded her more than a slam of the door could ever have done.

Putting a hand to her mouth, Kate stifled the moan that came to her lips. Tears burned in her eyes, but they did not fall. This pain was too deep, too profound for tears to wash away. She turned back to the window and the glass bowl caught her eye. Its wild color and beauty seemed to taunt her, to remind her of what she had just done. For a second, she was tempted to reach out and throw it against the wall.

Instead, she stumbled to the sofa and dropped to the cushions heavily. She drew herself into a ball, curving around the child growing in her belly. Slowly she began to rock, but the pain stayed lodged in her breast. She feared that this was one wound time would not heal. And she had thrust the knife in herself.

PATRICK PUSHED open the door to the office and stepped inside. "Where's Ian?"

His mother lifted a finger to hush him while she finished her call. She hung up and swiveled her chair to face him.

"Oh good, I was hoping you'd come back here today. I was just on the phone with Jeannie. Is Kate having a baby shower?"

"I don't know." Patrick's voice was flat. His temper was under the tightest of controls. "Where's Ian?"

Elaine rose and walked to the counter. "Find out for us, will—"

"Where's Ian?"

"Don't take that tone of voice with me, young man." Elaine frowned as she rebuked him. Her eyes searched his face and her expression went from angry to concerned. "What's wrong?"

"Nothing. I need to talk to Ian."

The front door opened and Patrick's brother stepped inside. "Man, it's still blowing like crazy out there."

"Can you drive me to the airport?" Patrick asked immediately.

"What are you talking about?"

"I need to catch the six o'clock flight to LAX."

Patrick's words were a bomb dropped into the room. His mother gasped. Ian grabbed his brother's arm. "You aren't really going, are you? Patty, I told you—"

"We have to leave now." Patrick had no interest in explaining. "I've got my gear bag in the back of the truck. Mom, here's the keys to the house, just in case. Nothing's been turned on there, so you don't have to do anything." He thrust a set of keys at his mother and turned back to Ian. "Let's go."

"Wait a minute. What the hell happened, Patty? What about Kate?"

Patrick stopped and sucked in a quick breath. He didn't

want to talk about the woman who had just ripped a hole
in his soul. "It's over," he said, simply. "I have to go."

Ian kept a hand on his arm and bored his eyes into
Patrick's. "What do you mean? What's over?"

"Kate and me." Patrick ran a hand through his hair.
"She never wants to see me again."

Elaine put a hand on the counter, as if to steady herself.
"What? Why would she say that? You were both just here.
And so happy." Her voice trailed off, bewildered.

"Yeah, well, we're not happy anymore," he said bitterly.
"I guess racing and being a father *don't* go together."

"What happened?" Ian asked.

"She heard about the race and she freaked." Patrick
spun away from the counter and looked out the window.
Stray pieces of paper and leaves swirled around the
parking lot.

"So tell her you won't do it, then."

"I did, but it doesn't matter." Patrick focused on his
brother again. "She's marrying Steve."

Elaine had been watching her sons, her lower lip caught
between her teeth. Her eyes darted first to one, then the
other. "What?" she whispered. "Who's Steve?"

"Shit," Ian murmured.

"She told me I'll never be a real father."

"But you *are* the father," Elaine said softly, her voice
full of tears.

Patrick swallowed hard. "Not anymore. I'm just the
sperm donor."

"I still think you should stay," Ian said. "At least a
couple of days. She might change her mind."

"Yes, please stay, Patrick." Elaine came around the
counter to take his hands, warm against the iciness of his
own flesh. "Kate is just upset right now. It's a very emotional time for her."

"No, Ma. I can't. It hurts too much." He put his arms around his mother and hugged her, offering comfort even while he took it from her. Her arms encircled him in the firm grip that had always helped him rise above the bumps and bruises life threw at him. This time, his pain did not abate. This was a hurt no one, not even a mother, could kiss and make better. "Watching her marry someone else is something I can't do. I need to leave for a while." He pulled back to look her in the eyes. "Maybe being at sea will make this whole thing clearer. Or at least get it out of my system."

A tear trickled down his mother's cheek. She stroked Patrick's chest once, then stepped back. "Be careful."

A wry smile twisted Patrick's lips. "I'm always careful."

He went out to his truck and climbed inside. Ian followed. They drove in silence to the airport. Patrick was glad Ian didn't ask more questions. There were no answers anyway. At the curbside check-in, Patrick got out and grabbed his bag from the back of the truck. Ian walked around to join him there and held out his hand. Patrick shook it firmly, then hugged his brother.

"See you."

Ian stepped back. He opened his mouth and closed it again, shaking his head.

"What?" Patrick asked. "You might as well say it."

"I don't think the ocean's going to give you any answers, Patty." Ian's words were quiet, nearly drowned out by the noise of buses, cars and people around them. "Not this time."

"What's to figure out? She's marrying someone else."

"She's not married yet."

Patrick hefted his bag. "All I know is that it's over."

Ian pressed his lips together in a tight line. "Well, do what you have to do. Good luck."

With a nod, Patrick turned away and stepped up onto the sidewalk, then stopped. He stood facing the wide glass windows for a long moment before finally turning around. "Hey, Ian?"

His brother hadn't moved. He still stood watching, with his hands in his pockets. "Yeah," he said. "I'll let you know."

Patrick nodded again, his throat too tight to speak. He spun around and walked through the automatic doors without a backward glance. The future was in front of him, waiting at a dock in Australia. The past didn't matter. Not now. Not ever.

Chapter Fourteen

Two hours after Patrick left, the knife-sharp pain inside Kate had not eased. The baby kicked and jabbed at her, echoing her agitation. After rocking in silent, tearless anguish, she pushed herself up from the sofa and paced from room to room trying to forget, but memories clamored at her everywhere she turned. She could not rest in the bedroom that held such fresh, sweet memories of love and tenderness. The living room reverberated with harsh words and shattered dreams.

Kate retreated to the kitchen to make a cup of chamomile tea, hoping the brew would soothe her troubled heart. When she turned to the table to sit, she stopped short at the sight of the newspaper stacked neatly where Patrick had left it. Suddenly, it was as if he were there bantering with her, teasing Molly, as he had done that morning.

She closed her eyes. All she saw was the tenderness in his face as he thanked her for the night before. She could almost feel his touch on her cheek. When she looked again, the room was empty. Her throat tightened and closed. Her eyes burned, but she would not cry. Shivering, Kate fled back to the living room with her tea.

She walked to the window, cradling the warm mug in

both hands. The wind still raged and now rain slapped against the glass panes in bursts of fitful temper. Lightning flashed in the southern sky not far away, followed by the low rumble of thunder. The garden was sodden, filled with dead leaves and tattered mums. It looked as cold and barren as Kate felt inside. There was no escape, no oasis.

She turned her back on the dreary scene, only to find herself staring at the bowl on the pedestal. Its bold, bright colors offered no solace, either. It reminded her too much of Patrick and the turbulence of their love. She traced a finger along the rim, lightly stroking the smooth glass inside, as if it were Patrick's skin.

The front door opened and closed with a bang. "Hello, anyone home?" Molly asked loudly.

Kate turned and her aunt came through the doorway, running a hand over her tousled hair. "It's miserable out there! I'll be glad when tropical depression Greta heads off to New England. Be careful on those steps, the wood is soaked and very slippery." Molly took off her wet jacket and dropped it on the rug at her feet. "I have some great news." She stopped short and peered at her niece's face. "What's wrong?"

"Nothing," Kate said evenly. She couldn't talk about what had happened. If she said Patrick's name aloud, she felt she would shatter into a thousand pieces.

"Was there a problem at the doctor's?" Molly's forehead creased in a frown. She walked over to Kate and stroked a hand down her cheek.

The tender touch was nearly Kate's undoing. The tears that had so stubbornly refused to fall earlier rose up like a flood tide. She blinked them back. "Everything went fine. The baby's doing great."

"But something's wrong," Molly said. "Is it Patrick?"

Kate shook her head. The mug in her hands started

shaking so hard she had to set it on the windowsill. "No. Not anymore."

"What does that mean?"

Kate pressed her fingertips against her closed lids for a second, then looked at her aunt. "He's gone."

"Gone?" Molly frowned again. "Gone where?"

"Australia."

"What? Whatever for?"

The tears would not be held back now. They welled up and, despite Kate's best efforts, slid down her face. She wiped them away with a trembling hand. "He's going to race."

"Race?" Molly stared at Kate, bewilderment written on her face. "Wait a minute. You're telling me that the man who was here this morning, the one who *couldn't take his eyes off you,* has gone to Australia?" Molly shook her head. "I don't believe it."

"It's true." Kate covered her face with her hands. In a muffled voice, she detailed what Patrick had been asked to do after the news of his friend's death. She dropped her hands. "So he went."

"I don't understand," Molly said, her face confused. "What did you say to him?"

"Me?" Kate stiffened. Tears still covered her cheeks. "You're blaming me?"

"I'm not blaming anyone," Molly said.

"It's not my fault that he left," Kate said, her voice sharp. "He *wanted* to go."

"But you're due in five weeks, Kate. It doesn't make sense."

"Why not? Because he's been so good at sticking around lately?" Kate flipped a hand out in a dismissive gesture and nearly upset the bowl on the pedestal beside her. She steadied it, her fingers curling around the edge for a second, then let go. "The past few weeks have been just a fantasy. *My* fantasy. The reality is that Patrick can't give up racing."

"He *has* been here for you, Katie," Molly said, arguing gently. "And he *is* a different man than when he got home in July. I've seen it and you have, too."

"No, he isn't," Kate said, biting each word off in anger. Anguish and rage filled her heart. "He won't change. He loves racing too much to give it up."

Molly watched her with concerned eyes. "He loves *you,* Kate."

Kate shook her head fiercely. "But not enough," she said through gritted teeth. "He loves danger *more.*"

In anger and fury, Kate swept the glass bowl off the pedestal. It hit the wall, then the floor, with a crash. Shards of red and gold glass sprayed out over the hardwood.

Molly gasped. "Oh, no!"

Kate stared openmouthed at the mess scattered across the living room floor, afraid to believe what she saw. She lifted dazed eyes to Molly's. With a hand to her cheek, Molly looked at Kate, her own eyes wide.

"What have I done?" Kate's eyes welled with tears again.

"It was an accident," Molly said softly.

"No." Kate shook her head slowly, looking down at the shattered glass. Tears began streaming unchecked down her face, falling to dampen her shirt. "No. It was no accident. I broke it because I was mad at Patrick. Or mad at myself. I lied to him."

"What?" Molly's brow furrowed. "What do you mean?"

Kate met her aunt's concerned eyes with her own tear-washed ones. "I told him I was marrying Steve."

"Kate, why?"

"I thought it was better that way. That I would feel

better when he left for good. When this was all over."
Kate hugged her arms around herself. "But I don't. I lied
and now he's gone and I feel worse than ever."

Molly stepped over to her niece, glass crunching under
her feet, to enfold her in a warm embrace. "It'll be all right,
Katie."

Kate rested her head against the older woman's shoulder. She wanted to take comfort from the embrace, but the
vast emptiness inside her refused to allow it. Only one
person could fill that abyss. She pulled back and looked
into her aunt's eyes.

"I have to see Patrick."

"Not tonight. It's not safe to travel. Why don't you
just call him?"

Kate shook her head fiercely. "I'll take my phone and
try to call in the car. But I have to see him in person."

"But—"

"I have to tell Patrick the truth. About Steve and about
how I feel. That I...I love him. I owe him that much at
least." Kate swallowed hard. "Then he can make his own
decision. He'll go. Or he'll stay."

The two women's gazes met and held. Molly must have
read the determination in Kate's eyes. She didn't protest
anymore. "Then let me drive. I won't stay here and worry
about you on a night like this."

"Thank you." Kate laid a hand against her aunt's cheek.

"Wait here. I'll get my car." Molly patted Kate's arm,
then went across the room to where she had dropped her
raincoat and slipped into it. As she pulled open the front
door, a burst of wind slashed rain into her face. "We both
must be crazy," she muttered.

Kate followed her to the hall and reached into the closet
for a long raincoat. When the tan fabric wouldn't button
over her girth, she grabbed an umbrella for additional pro-

tection. Gathering up her purse and her keys, she went back into the living room, ignoring the glass under her feet, and peered through the window that looked out over the alley. When Molly's red SUV appeared, Kate made her way back to the front door and went outside.

The rain beat against her immediately and the wind whipped her hair around her head. She yanked the door shut behind her and opened the umbrella. A gust nearly ripped it from her hands. Taking a tighter grip on the handle, she angled it into the wind to protect her face. As she took the first step down, another gust caught the umbrella. The force pulled Kate off balance. Her purse tumbled out of her other hand, and her feet slipped on the wet wood.

Kate grabbed for the railing, but it was too late. She fell heavily onto her side, twisting to keep the bulk of her belly from hitting the edges of the steps. A sharp pain stabbed through her and she cried out. Then her head hit something hard and the world turned gray, then slowly black.

PATRICK RUBBED a hand over his face and pushed two fingers against his gritty eyes. Seated at the rear of the crowded plane, he was cramped, uncomfortable and tired.

Mostly, he was heartbroken.

He tried to ignore the empty feeling in his chest. His MP3 player kept a constant stream of rock and roll flowing into his ears. He thumbed through the stack of sailing magazines he had brought and studied his planning charts for the Indian Ocean. He reviewed the specs for the boat and the weather reports that Chris had e-mailed. He did all the things he usually did to prepare himself for a race. Nothing worked.

The past few months had changed him more than he

ever thought possible. How had he ever spent three months away from Kate and only had contact with her once? It was inconceivable. Now, three *hours* away from her seemed like an agonizing trial. And he had sold his boat and bought a house without one pang of regret. What more proof did he need? He was a different man whose heart was filled with a yearning for one woman and the child she carried. Bashing across the ocean, pushing for every ounce of speed a boat could give, placed a distant third in the things that mattered most to him.

He fidgeted in his seat, anxious for the flight to be over. What difference it made, he didn't know. He would just be getting on another plane for a longer flight when this one reached L.A. Kate was lost to him now. He loved her, but she would never know it. Soon she would marry Steve and start a new life. Patrick swallowed hard. The ache in his heart grew with every mile he traveled away from her. He would have to learn to live with that pain now; there was no hope of reprieve.

Closing his eyes, Patrick tried once more to sleep, but all the things he wanted to say to Kate circled through his head, keeping him awake. What would he say? Mostly just the simple truth. He needed her. He loved her. He sighed, opening his eyes again, and reached for another magazine. He would have to get some rest on the long flight to Melbourne.

When they landed in Los Angeles, Patrick filed off the plane with the rest of the passengers. As he followed them up the jet way, he turned on his cell phone and checked his messages. His heart started beating fast when he saw Kate's number listed as a missed call. There was also one voice mail.

Patrick stopped stock-still in the middle of the hallway and punched in the code to retrieve it. A man with a brief-case and a roller bag swerved around him with a muttered curse. Patrick passed through the gate, pushed only by the momentum of other passengers. He held his breath, waiting to hear Kate's voice. A woman's voice sounded, breathless and hoarse. But it wasn't Kate.

"Patrick. It's Molly. Kate had an accident. We're at Arundel Medical Center. Please call me back as soon as you get this message."

Patrick dropped the phone away from his ear as it beeped and the voice prompt asked him if he wanted to save the message or delete it. He stopped again, stunned by the report. People streamed past him on both sides, the airport concourse busy even at this late hour. He hit the redial button. Kate did not answer. Overhead, he heard a woman's voice announcing a departure.

"Flight five-two-two with nonstop service to Dulles International Airport is now in final boarding at gate C thirty-four. All passengers should make their way to gate C thirty-four now, for an on-time departure."

The voice over the loudspeaker sent a shock through Patrick's mind. He looked up, wildly searching for the gate number he had just exited: C 11. Gate C 10 lay just ahead. Without leaving a message, he closed the phone and spun around, nearly plowing into a large man in cowboy boots and a Stetson.

"Watch it, son!"

"Sorry. I have to catch a plane!"

The man's answer went unheard as Patrick raced down the corridor, dodging people, luggage and carts as he ran. He heard another announcement for the flight just as he slid to a stop at the check-in counter. He shoved his phone into a pocket and pulled out his wallet, fumbling for his credit card. A burly man in a burgundy jacket and tie looked up at him over the top of his half-glasses.

"Please, get me on this flight."

"Sir, we're just about—"

"Please," Patrick interrupted. "I just found out that the woman I love was in an accident. She's eight months' pregnant. I have to get back to the East Coast as soon as possible."

The man stared at him for a moment, then his fingers began to tap the keyboard in front of him. He muttered a few words into a handheld radio before looking at Patrick again. "It's gonna be expensive."

"I don't care," Patrick said, drawing in a deep breath.

The man took his credit card, tapped, muttered some more and soon pulled a boarding pass out of the printer behind the counter. Handing it and the credit card to Patrick, he said, "Sign here." Then he pointed to a woman in a blue nylon jacket speaking into another radio. "Give this to the lady at that door."

"Thanks, man."

The man smiled dourly and Patrick rushed to the gate agent. She scanned his pass and, minutes later, he was seated. He pulled his phone out and dialed Kate's number again. There was no answer this time, either. His fingers tapped the armrest as he waited for the signal to begin his message.

"Kate, I'm on my way home from LAX. The plane's leaving right now. I'll be there as soon as I can." He paused for a second as the flight attendant asked everyone to turn off their cell phones. "I have to hang up now. I love you, Kate."

He pressed the off button and the screen went black. The plane rolled onto the runway as he squeezed the small, gray device in his hand. Seconds later, he was airborne. All through the flight, Patrick held the phone like a talisman. Kate and the baby had to be all right. They had to be. He closed his eyes and willed the plane to fly faster.

Chapter Fifteen

The hospital room was dark except for the glow of the monitors. Kate lay on her side in the high bed. Wires connecting her to the machines looked like a black web in the gloom. The small pads adhered to her stomach made her skin itch, but she ignored the irritation. Despite her tiredness and the ache in her head, she intently watched the screens at her bedside.

One in particular held her attention: the monitor for the baby's heartbeat. Each blip was a tiny reassurance, but Kate still had both of her hands spread wide over the mound of her stomach. Every few minutes, she slid her hands to a different place, hoping to feel the quick kick or soft pat of the baby inside her. A litany, a prayer, a desperate cry ran over and over in her head: *please move*. She blinked back tears when she felt nothing.

The door opened and a figure came in quietly. Molly sat down beside the bed and laid one of her hands over Kate's. "How are you?" she asked in a soft voice.

"She still hasn't moved." Kate's eyes remained trained on the monitors.

"The doctors said the baby had a shock, Katie. That's all. The heartbeat is still strong." Molly squeezed her niece's hand. "She'll move when she's ready."

"I tried so hard not to fall on her, but what if—"

"Kate." Molly lifted the hand she held and kissed it. "Don't blame yourself. Things like this happen. She'll be fine. Now you need to relax and rest. You're not doing the baby any good by lying here and worrying."

"But—"

"But nothing." The older woman's tone was firm. "Close your eyes and rest for a while. I'll watch the monitors."

Reluctantly, Kate did as she was told. She knew Molly was right, but it was so hard not to worry when the baby had not kicked or squirmed since the fall down the steps. The doctors were keeping Kate in the hospital for observation. She felt helpless, lying in bed, waiting, hoping for a sign. She shifted to a more comfortable position, pulling the pillow farther under the weight of her belly. She wished she had Patrick to rest against.

"Did you talk to him?" Kate asked, her eyes still closed.

Molly didn't have to ask who she meant. "Not yet."

The reply stabbed at Kate. "He's probably halfway to Australia."

A tear slid from her eye to dampen the pillowcase beneath her cheek. When Patrick had not returned Molly's first call, Kate had asked her aunt to call his brother. Ian told them Patrick was already on a plane. He promised he would get a message to him whenever he could. If all else failed, he could call Chris in Melbourne who would see Patrick when he arrived at the boat.

The news lowered Kate's spirits even further. She hadn't caught him before he left. She wondered how long it would be before she saw him again. Maybe never. The longer he was gone, the less likely it was that she could reverse the damage her lie had made. She had smashed a thing precious beyond imagining.

"I'm sure Patrick will call when he can," Molly assured her. "Ian will get through to him."

"What if he doesn't want to call?" The words burst out of Kate before she could stop them. She bit her lip and clutched her aunt's hand tightly. "Oh, Molly. What have I done?"

Leaning over the tall bed, Molly took Kate in a warm embrace. She stroked a hand over her niece's tousled hair and, for once, had nothing to say.

Kate nestled against the older woman, closed her eyes and took a deep breath. She needed Patrick with her, now more than ever, but he was gone, heading for the other side of the world. She didn't want to face the future without him. Especially a future that seemed so dark and hollow.

AS SOON AS THE PLANE touched down, Patrick was on the phone. He checked his voice mail and found a message from Ian waiting.

"Patty. Kate's okay, but she slipped and fell on the steps outside her house and knocked herself out. No concussion or anything, just a bump on the head and some bruises. They're keeping her in the hospital overnight for observation, just to be sure about the baby. I'm going to call Chris and leave the same message there." Ian paused for a second. "Get on a plane home as soon as you can. You need to be here."

"I'm already here, bro," Patrick muttered to himself.

He closed the phone and waited impatiently for the plane to dock at a gate. As soon as the way was clear, he was running through the airport to the taxi stand. Once underway, he called Kate's cell phone, but it went directly to voice mail. Molly's did the same. He left messages on both, then called directory assistance and got through to Arundel Medical Center. No one would give him any information except that Miss Stevens was resting comfortably. They wouldn't connect him to her room, either, since it was six-thirty in the morning.

Patrick ended the call with a muttered oath. The cab slowed to a crawl as it hit the morning commute on the beltway around Washington, D.C. Patrick tried to be patient, dialing Ian's number.

His brother answered on the second ring. "Hey. Did you get my message? You need to get home—"

"I know," Patrick interrupted. "I'm there, or nearly." He rubbed his bleary eyes. Running a hand through his hair, he looked at the maddening traffic around the taxicab. "I had to fly into Dulles and I'm stuck on the beltway. Have you heard anything about Kate?"

"Not this morning. I was at the hospital last night and she was resting."

"And the baby?"

There was a long pause. "I think it's going to be okay."

"What are you saying, Ian?" Patrick's throat tightened. "Is there a problem?"

"I don't know, Patty." His brother sighed. "The heartbeat's strong, but…the baby wasn't moving last night."

"Does that mean—"

"Don't even think it," Ian said forcefully. "They're both going to be fine. The doctors are monitoring everything and they'd have told us if there was a real problem."

Patrick sat back and ran a hand over his face. He had an awful feeling in the pit of his stomach. "I hope you're right."

"Me, too."

"Look, I'm going directly to the hospital. I'll catch up to you after I see Kate."

"I'm going there this morning, too, with Ma and Pop. They went last night, but the doctors wouldn't let them stay long."

"I bet Ma loved that."

"Pop didn't have to drag her out of there kicking and screaming, but it was close. She had that look she gets." Ian chuckled. "I'll see you later."

"See you."

Patrick closed the phone and leaned forward to put his head in his hands. He was exhausted from lack of sleep and worry about Kate. It sickened him that he had been on a plane when this happened. Ian's words didn't help as they whirled around in Patrick's head, making him even queasier. Though he couldn't have done anything to stop the accident, he still blamed himself for being gone when it happened.

Kate might blame him, too.

For the first time since he had decided to turn around and come home, Patrick forced himself to consider the fact that Kate probably wouldn't want him there. She had banished him from her life less than twenty-four hours ago. It was unlikely that she had suddenly changed her mind. Yes, she had fallen, but that didn't mean she needed *him*. No one had said, "Kate wants you to come home."

Who was with her now? Molly certainly. Steve, too? The idea burned in Patrick's heart, but he had to admit that it was probably true. He sat up as the cab turned a sharp corner and he finally saw the hospital looming ahead. Exhaustion fell away as adrenaline surged. The cab pulled up to the front door and Patrick paid the man, adding a generous tip, then dashed through the revolving door into the lobby. He decided that it didn't matter who had been with Kate last night. What mattered was that *he* was going to be with her now.

THE DOOR MADE A SOFT HUSHING sound as it opened. Kate kept her eyes closed. She didn't want to see or talk to anyone. She had drifted in and out of sleep during the long tortuous night, without getting any real rest. The monitors still blipped beside her, counting out the steady heart-beats. The litany in her head had softened to a gentle plea that had gone unanswered. There was still no movement from the small life she carried within her.

A callused hand stroked over her cheek, pushing her hair away from her face. Kate's eyes flew open to see Patrick standing next to her bed. She blinked once, then twice, certain she must be dreaming.

"But you're in Australia!" she said, bewildered.

"No, I'm not." He smiled slightly, his silver eyes capturing hers. "I'm right here where I belong, Katie."

With a cry of welcome, Kate reached out her arms and was wrapped in his strong embrace. His heavily whiskered face scratched her soft skin and she pressed against him harder. She couldn't believe he had returned, that he held her.

Patrick pulled back first. He put one hand gently on her stomach, fingers spread wide. "How is she?"

Tears welled in Kate's eyes. "I don't know. Oh, Patrick, she hasn't moved since I fell last night. I'm so scared that—"

"No, don't say it," he said, pressing a finger to her lips. "She's just resting. That's what we have to believe. You must have taken quite a tumble."

"I was coming to find you, to tell you I was..." Her words trailed off as Patrick paled and closed his eyes. "What's wrong?"

"It *was* my fault," he whispered.

"No! It was an accident."

"But if I hadn't left—"

"Listen to me, Patrick." Kate cupped one bristled cheek in her hand and turned his face to hers. "It's no one's fault."

She swallowed hard. "I'm trying not to blame myself, either. I know it's hard, but I've been thinking about it all night. You were right. Accidents happen. That's how life goes sometimes. I can't stop the bad things. Neither can you. We can only keep praying that she's going to be all right."

"She will be. She has to be." Patrick pressed a soft kiss to her lips, then went around to the other side of the bed and dropped the steel gate. Kicking off his shoes, he tossed his jacket to the floor and climbed up onto the mattress with her. There was barely enough room, but they managed, Patrick curling around Kate and pulling her close. Once he was settled, he kissed her and fit her head onto his shoulder. A large hand caressed her belly.

Kate savored the warmth of his embrace. She felt that a piece of her had finally slid into its rightful place. With Patrick home, holding her so sweetly, she began to believe that somehow they would be all right. Whatever happened, she had a family, right here in this bed.

Pulling back a little, she searched his eyes. "Will you forgive me? I lied about marrying Steve. I haven't even *seen* him in weeks. I thought that if I pushed you away I wouldn't get hurt, that I'd be happier, but I wasn't. I'm never going to be happy without you."

Patrick took her mouth in a soft kiss. "There's nothing to forgive. Last night, alone on that plane, I realized how much you mean to me, too. I love you, Katie. With all my heart."

His words took her by surprise. She closed her eyes tightly for a second, then opened them to see if her fantasy had really come true. "Oh, Patrick. I love you, too."

He kissed her again, harder this time. Kate was breathless, returning every kiss and caress, unable to believe that he forgave her and loved her.

"I wanted you here," she whispered between kisses. "I needed you, Patrick."

"I'm glad," he said quietly, his eyes dark. "I was afraid you wouldn't want me."

"I'll always need you with me," Kate said. She stroked a hand across his cheek and back into his curling hair. "But I know you need to go away sometimes, too. I'll wait for you. *We'll* wait for you, as long as it takes."

Their fingers laced together on top of her stomach. Just then, a hard thump hit their palms, sending a vibration through Kate's soul. She turned wide eyes to Patrick. He looked just as shocked. Then a grin split his face. When he laughed, she joined him. Happiness flooded her, joy making her delirious. Another push from the baby inside sent tears cascading down her cheeks.

"She's awake and happy you're home." Kate's voice was thick with tears of joy.

"And she knows that's where I'm going to stay."

"Patrick—"

He stopped her words with a kiss. "I love you, Kate. More than *anything*."

His mouth dropped to hers again. His kiss promised love and fidelity. It was punctuated by the small kicks from the life they had created together. Kate's heart swelled. She would never be alone again, not as long as Patrick loved her. The future was theirs. Together.

Epilogue

With a splash, the anchor dropped off the bow of the boat and into the water. Patrick signaled her to reverse the engine and Kate pulled the control lever carefully. Minutes later, he gave her a thumbs-up, signaling that the anchor had dug in and she put the engine in neutral, then turned it off. The peace and quiet of the tiny anchorage was broken only by the sound of a dog barking on shore and a happy babble from the baby in a car seat across from her.

Patrick stepped into the cockpit and sat down next to Kate. He gave the baby a kiss and a tickle, making her giggle and squeal.

"What is this?" Kate complained. "I'm the one who drove us in here and she gets all the attention?"

Patrick grinned. "Piloted, sweetheart, not 'drove.'" He kissed Kate lightly, sliding his arms around her, then drew back a little to look into her eyes. "You did a great job."

"Thank you." Kate preened a bit, patting herself on the back in mock congratulation.

With a laugh, Patrick hugged her close. "You deserve a reward."

One of his hands came up to tangle in her hair, dragging her head back for a much longer, much more complicated kiss than before. Kate leaned into him, running her fingers over his shoulders, feeling the muscles flex and bunch. Her arms twined around his neck as she lost herself in his kiss and his touch. The baby's howl brought his head up. They looked over at their daughter, frowning at them with a tear trembling on one lash.

Patrick kept one arm around Kate and reached out a finger that was immediately clasped. "Jealous, Betsy-Wetsy?"

"Don't call her that," Kate said, but she couldn't help laughing at the nickname sometimes. "She'll hate you when she's a teenager."

"Oh, don't worry," he said. "Evan will have thought of something much worse to call her by then."

They both laughed, thinking the same thing: poor Evan.

The extremely reluctant godfather was at a complete loss around the baby. He had agreed to play the honorary role at Patrick's request, but refused to actually have anything to do with the small, wriggling girl. He had taken one look at her, cocked a blond eyebrow and declared that he would be affectionate from a distance. A safe distance of about twenty yards.

His vow had no effect at all on his goddaughter. Elizabeth Elaine Berzani adored him. No one could figure out why, but, whenever Evan was around, the baby fussed and squirmed until he picked her up. The first time he did so, he discovered that she had a very wet diaper and he had christened her with Betsy-Wetsy.

Patrick turned back to Kate and rested his forehead against hers. "Looks like I'll have to reward you later, when the baby's asleep."

A shiver slid over her skin at the promise in her husband's eyes. "I can't wait to get my prize," she said with a smile.

With one final squeeze, Patrick slipped away. He rose

and started coiling lines in the cockpit while Kate reached over to lift Beth from her car seat. She and her daughter had both done well today out on the water. Of course, Beth had no fears to overcome. She loved being so close to her parents and the constant rock of the boat kept her dozing most of the time.

Patrick was careful with them both, too. He and Kate had been out several times for gentle sails near the marina. Granny Elaine had been more than happy to look after her latest grandchild for an hour or two. Slowly, Kate had come to understand why Patrick loved the water so much. She didn't think she would ever want to ride one of the beasts he was so fond of over the middle of the ocean, but she feared much less for him when he did.

His "beasts," as she called them, weren't quite so large these days. Patrick had given up long-distance racing, even though she had tried to talk him out of it. He told her that he needed to be at home with her and Beth more than he needed the open sea. Their argument ranged back and forth until he told her he wasn't giving up racing completely, just the longer ones. He was now active in local one-design racing and had plans for a bid at a national title. Evan was one of his partners on the boat and they had already blasted most of the nearby competition out of the water. Kate shook her head resolutely every time Evan invited her along. His wicked grin was enough to keep her far from any boat he was sailing.

Patrick, she trusted. She had discovered he was a careful and attentive sailor at all times. Watching him move effortlessly around the boat, she was awed by his easy skill. And aroused. She had even seduced him one warm spring afternoon on the boat, much to his delight. He teased her about it often, offering, with a wink and a nudge, to take her sailing. Kate laughed and blushed and sometimes took him up on the offer.

This was their second overnight outing on the boat. The weather was perfect and the winds gentle enough that Kate felt comfortable having Beth with them. Buckled into her car seat, which was lashed to the bench in the cockpit, she wasn't in any danger. Nonetheless, Patrick let Kate's comfort level determine their plans. If she didn't like the weather or seas, they stayed in harbor. She was grateful to him for that. He had turned out to be the husband she had dreamed of—the very one she had planned for all those months ago. Kate sometimes mused that if she hadn't made her plans, they might have gotten to this happiness much sooner.

Their wedding at Christmas had been lovely and huge. Kate had focused on her new baby and let Molly and Elaine orchestrate the entire event. The two women had done a wonderful job. The entire Berzani clan attended, along with Patrick and Kate's many friends. Kate's father and mother had flown in for a few hours, but were gone before the cake was cut. Patrick was furious, but Kate wasn't. She simply kissed her husband and told him she had all the family she needed now. Antonio and Elaine had chosen that moment to sweep up and claim a dance from the newlyweds. Kate laughed and mouthed a *see-I-told-you-so* to Patrick as she spun away with her new father-in-law. Patrick shook his head and led his mother out onto the floor, as well.

Steve had forgiven her and attended the wedding, too. Grateful for his kindness and deeply sorry for the hurt she had caused, she was relieved when he and Suzanne from the coffee shop hit it off at the reception and danced the night away. The pair were dating now and Steve was happier than he had ever been with Kate.

Cockpit tidy, Patrick disappeared down below. Just as

Beth began to fret, he handed up a bottle of warm milk. Kate was unsurprised by his prescience. As good as he was at being a husband, he was a better father. He was usually the first up in the middle of the night, sometimes before Kate even heard Beth fuss. He also liked to take the baby with him on errands, tucking her securely in a belly pack or into the car seat in his truck and talking to her all the while.

She cuddled Beth into the crook of her arm and popped the nipple in her mouth. Unfortunately, Kate hadn't been able to produce enough milk, so she used a bottle and formula after the first few weeks. Beth slurped down dinner as Kate leaned back with a sigh of contentment.

Patrick reappeared with an open bottle of wine and two glasses. "A bottle for the mother, too, my dear?"

Kate murmured her agreement and he poured them each a glass. Setting the bottle aside, he settled into place beside her, and Kate leaned into his embracing arm. Beth watched them both solemnly as they touched glasses, kissed and then sipped the mellow wine. The sun dropped slowly behind the trees as the boat gently rocked them.

Kate sighed and nestled closer to Patrick, feeling the joy and happiness that seemed to flood her almost every day. Love, spun as fine and beautiful as one of her glass orbs, annealed in the heat of adversity, sparkled all around them. Together, they would keep a fire burning in the crucible of their hearts, shaping and strengthening their love into a beautiful creation.

* * * * *

*Celebrate 60 years of pure reading pleasure
with Harlequin® Books!*

*Harlequin Romance® is celebrating by showering you
with* DIAMOND BRIDES *in February 2009.
Six stories that promise to bring a touch of sparkle to
your life, with diamond proposals and dazzling
weddings, sparkling brides and gorgeous grooms!*

Enjoy a sneak peek at Caroline Anderson's
TWO LITTLE MIRACLES,
available February 2009 from Harlequin Romance®.

'I've FOUND HER.'

Max froze.

It was what he'd been waiting for since June, but now—now he was almost afraid to voice the question. His heart stalling, he leaned slowly back in his chair and scoured the investigator's face for clues. 'Where?' he asked, and his voice sounded rough and unused, like a rusty hinge.

'In Suffolk. She's living in a cottage.'

Living. His heart crashed back to life, and he sucked in a long, slow breath. All these months he'd feared—

'Is she well?'

'Yes, she's well.'

He had to force himself to ask the next question. 'Alone?'

The man paused. 'No. The cottage belongs to a man called John Blake. He's working away at the moment, but he comes and goes.'

God. He felt sick. So sick he hardly registered the next few words, but then gradually they sank in. 'She's got *what?*'

'Babies. Twin girls. They're eight months old.'

'Eight—?' he echoed under his breath. 'They must be his.'

He was thinking out loud, but the P.I. heard and corrected him.

'Apparently not. I gather they're hers. She's been there since mid-January last year, and they were born during the summer—June, the woman in the post office thought. She was more than helpful. I think there's been a certain amount of speculation about their relationship.'

He'd just bet there had. God, he was going to kill her. Or Blake. Maybe both of them.

'Of course, looking at the dates, she was presumably pregnant when she left you, so they could be yours, or she could have been having an affair with this Blake character...'

He glared at the unfortunate P.I. 'Just stick to your job. I can do the math,' he snapped, swallowing the unpalatable possibility that she'd been unfaithful to him before she'd left. 'Where is she? I want the address.'

'It's all in here,' the man said, sliding a large envelope across the desk to him. 'With my invoice.'

'I'll get it seen to. Thank you.'

'If there's anything else you need, Mr Gallagher, any further information—'

'I'll be in touch.'

'The woman in the post office told me Blake was away at the moment, if that helps,' he added quietly, and opened the door.

Max stared down at the envelope, hardly daring to open it, but when the door clicked softly shut behind the P.I., he eased up the flap, tipped it and felt his breath jam in his throat as the photos spilled out over the desk.

Oh, lord, she looked gorgeous. Different, though. It took him a moment to recognise her, because she'd grown her hair, and it was tied back in a ponytail, making her look younger and somehow freer. The blond highlights were gone, and it was back to its natural soft golden-brown, with a little curl in the end of the ponytail that he wanted to thread his finger through and tug, just gently, to draw her back to him.

Crazy. She'd put on a little weight, but it suited her. She looked well and happy and beautiful, but oddly, considering how desperate he'd been for news of her for the past year—one year, three weeks and two days, to be exact—it wasn't only Julia who held his attention after the initial shock. It was the babies sitting side by side in a supermarket trolley. Two identical and absolutely beautiful little girls.

* * * * *

When Max Gallagher hires a P.I. to find his estranged wife, Julia, he discovers she's not alone—she has twin baby girls, and they might be his. Now workaholic Max has just two weeks to prove that he can be a wonderful husband and father to the family he wants to treasure.

Look for TWO LITTLE MIRACLES
by Caroline Anderson,
available February 2009
from Harlequin Romance®

CELEBRATE
60 YEARS
OF PURE READING PLEASURE
WITH HARLEQUIN®!

**We'll be spotlighting a different series
every month throughout 2009
to celebrate our 60th anniversary.**

Look for Harlequin® Romance in February!

**Harlequin® Romance is celebrating by showering
you with Diamond Brides in February 2009.**

Six stories that promise to bring a touch of sparkle to
your life, with diamond proposals and dazzling weddings,
sparkling brides and gorgeous grooms!

Collect all six books in February 2009,
featuring *Two Little Miracles* by Caroline Anderson.

*Look for the Diamond Brides miniseries
in February 2009!*

www.eHarlequin.com   HRBRIDES09

HARLEQUIN® *Romance*®

This February the Harlequin® Romance series
will feature six Diamond Brides stories featuring
diamond proposals and gorgeous grooms.

Share your dream wedding proposal and you could WIN!

The most romantic entry will win a diamond
necklace and will inspire a proposal in one of
our upcoming Diamond Grooms books in 2010.

In 100 words or less, tell us the most romantic
way that you dream of being proposed to.

For more information, and to enter
the Diamond Brides Proposal contest, please visit
www.DiamondBridesProposal.com

Or mail your entry to us at:

IN THE U.S.: 3010 Walden Ave., P.O. Box 9069, Buffalo, NY 14269-9069
IN CANADA: 225 Duncan Mill Road, Don Mills, ON M3B 3K9

REQUEST YOUR FREE BOOKS!
2 FREE NOVELS PLUS 2
FREE GIFTS!

Love, Home & Happiness!

YES! Please send me 2 FREE Harlequin® American Romance® novels and my 2 FREE gifts (gifts are worth about $10). After receiving them, if I don't wish to receive any more books, I can return the shipping statement marked "cancel." If I don't cancel, I will receive 4 brand-new novels every month and be billed just $4.24 per book in the U.S. or $4.99 per book in Canada. That's a savings of close to 15% off the cover price! It's quite a bargain! Shipping and handling is just 25¢ per book, along with any applicable taxes.* I understand that accepting the 2 free books and gifts places me under no obligation to buy anything. I can always return a shipment and cancel at any time. Even if I never buy another book from Harlequin, the two free books and gifts are mine to keep forever.

154 HDN EEZK 354 HDN EEZV

Name	(PLEASE PRINT)

Address		Apt. #

City	State/Prov.	Zip/Postal Code

Signature (if under 18, a parent or guardian must sign)

Mail to the Harlequin Reader Service:
IN U.S.A.: P.O. Box 1867, Buffalo, NY 14240-1867
IN CANADA: P.O. Box 609, Fort Erie, Ontario L2A 5X3

Not valid to current subscribers of Harlequin® American Romance® books.

Want to try two free books from another line?
Call 1-800-873-8635 or visit www.morefreebooks.com.

* Terms and prices subject to change without notice. N.Y. residents add applicable sales tax. Canadian residents will be charged applicable provincial taxes and GST. Offer not valid in Quebec. This offer is limited to one order per household. All orders subject to approval. Credit or debit balances in a customer's account(s) may be offset by any other outstanding balance owed by or to the customer. Please allow 4 to 6 weeks for delivery. Offer available while quantities last.

Your Privacy: Harlequin is committed to protecting your privacy. Our Privacy Policy is available online at www.eHarlequin.com or upon request from the Reader Service. From time to time we make our lists of customers available to reputable third parties who may have a product or service of interest to you. If you would prefer we not share your name and address, please check here. ☐

HAR08R2

You're invited to join our Tell Harlequin Reader Panel!

By joining our new reader panel you will:

- Receive Harlequin® books—they are FREE and yours to keep with no obligation to purchase anything!
- Participate in fun online surveys
- Exchange opinions and ideas with women just like you
- Have a say in our new book ideas and help us publish the best in women's fiction

In addition, you will have a chance to win great prizes and receive special gifts! See Web site for details. Some conditions apply. Space is limited.

To join, visit us at
www.TellHarlequin.com.

Inside ROMANCE

Stay up-to-date on all your romance reading news!

The Inside Romance newsletter is a FREE quarterly newsletter highlighting our upcoming series releases and promotions!

Click on the <u>Inside Romance</u> link on the front page of **www.eHarlequin.com** or e-mail us at insideromance@harlequin.ca to sign up to receive your FREE newsletter today!

You can also subscribe by writing us at: HARLEQUIN BOOKS
Attention: Customer Service Department
P.O. Box 9057, Buffalo, NY 14269-9057

Please allow 4-6 weeks for delivery of the first issue by mail.

IRNBPA208

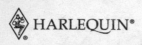

HARLEQUIN®

American ★ Romance®

COMING NEXT MONTH

#1245 ONCE A LAWMAN by Lisa Childs
Men Made in America
To protect and serve is the credo Chad Michalski has always lived by. But who's going to protect *him* from the vivacious blonde he just pulled over for speeding? Tessa Howard's recklessness has landed her in the Lakewood Citizens Police Academy, where the widowed cop can keep a close eye on her...and fight a losing battle against their growing attraction.

#1246 THE SECRET AGENT'S SURPRISES by Tina Leonard
The Morgan Men
Secret agent Pete Morgan has never considered himself a family man. Until he returns to Texas to collect his inheritance...and meets quadruplet babies in need of a home. To adopt the four tiny angels, Pete needs a wife. Prim, proper and wildly attractive Priscilla Perkins is the perfect candidate. Besides, it's just a temporary engagement. *Isn't it?*

#1247 ONCE UPON A VALENTINE'S by Holly Jacobs
American Dads
Single mom Carly Lewis thinks it's oh-so-ironic that she's organizing the local school's Valentine's Day dance! Cue the music *and* hunky Lieutenant Chuck Jefferson, the good-natured cop who wears his badge proudly on his chest and his heart on his sleeve. They've each been burned by love, so Cupid's working overtime this holiday to show these two how special they are together....

#1248 THE MAN SHE MARRIED by Ann DeFee
Maizie Walker is in a funk. After twenty years of marriage, all she wants is a little more attention from her husband, Clay. What's a girl to do? Make him jealous, of course! Maizie's convinced that flirting with another man will make Clay sit up and take notice. But when her plan backfires and Clay moves out, can Maizie ever get him back?

www.eHarlequin.com

HARCNMBPA0109